COWBOYS DON'T MARRY THEIR ENEMY

First edition. October 23, 2019.

Written by Jessie Gussman.

D1707766

Cover art by Brenda Walter https://bluevalleyauthorservices.site/

Editing by Heather Hayden https://hhaydeneditor.com/

Narration by Jay Dyess https://www.acx.com/narrator?p=A3VWKVSC6MFZHW

Click HERE[1] if you'd like to subscribe to my newsletter and find out why people say "Jessie's is the only newsletter I open and read." And "You make my day brighter. Love, love, love reading your newsletters. I don't know where you find time to write books. You are so busy living life. A true blessing." And "I know from now on that I can't be drinking my morning coffee while reading your newsletter – I laughed so hard I sprayed it out all over the table!"

---

1.   https://BookHip.com/FASFD

Chapter 1

When Abner Coblantz lived in southern Ohio, just across the Ohio River from Kentucky and West Virginia, he'd thought the winters were cold.

After having spent a winter in North Dakota, he'd changed his mind.

Ohio wasn't cold.

It was brown. It had more curves than a wrinkled blanket. And not only did it make him carsick to drive his Harley over the hills and valleys and hairpin turns, but the deeper he went into the redneck hill country of his childhood, the closer he got to the Amish community where he'd spent the first thirteen years of his life and the tiny towns where he'd lived out the rest of his miserable childhood, the more he wanted to turn his bike around and put it in the wind.

So, of course, he didn't.

His first thirteen years had taught him self-control and self-denial. The rest of his life had tested that teaching.

He could eat what others couldn't, work when others dropped, and smile through pain that would have another man on his knees.

But he hadn't wanted to test his limits by coming back to his hometown and risking running into the girl he hated. And loved.

Until today.

His gram had died. His mother wanted to see him. And his half-brother, who'd been involved with everything up to his eyeballs, had swallowed his pride and called Abner.

So, here he was.

He'd parked his bike at the church that was a staple in the center of every town in the northeast and walked three houses down.

2

It wasn't the house he'd grown up in. There'd been about seven or eight houses after he'd left the Amish. None of them had been this one. Still, this was the address in the paper where, in lieu of flowers, donations to help cover funeral expenses could be sent. It might not be his mother's house, but he'd not called to check.

He wasn't giving them a warning.

He'd found his way here, and he could find his way home, and if he didn't see anyone he knew in the meantime, he wouldn't be heartbroken.

Couldn't break something that had never been fixed.

A big, old oak, with tangled branches bare against the low, bereaved gray sky, squatted in the front yard. A white picket fence, missing most of the pickets, looking more dull, chipped gray than white, and using a very liberal definition of the word "fence," lined the cracked and broken sidewalk. Other derelict homes in various states of neglect hunkered along the street.

Broken toys, faded plastic garbage and tired lawn decorations dotted the small yards between the sidewalk and the structures.

The walk was just a path through the front yard to the house, or maybe there were stones under the weeds and dried grass. He couldn't tell.

Before he'd moved the broken gate out of the way, the front door burst open and two boys rushed out, yelling and grabbing at each other, leaving the door hanging open behind them. One was slightly bigger than the other, and they both looked to be elementary school age. About the same age as Gina, his harvest crew boss's daughter.

The boys never even saw him but jumped the steps in one leap and tore around the side of the house.

Abner watched, his heart beating slow and heavy in his throat. One of those boys could have been the baby Cora was carrying when he left. The one she claimed was his.

The one they both knew wasn't.

He pushed the aching pressure aside. He'd never been so hurt himself and angry at another human as he had been with Cora when all that went down.

He'd had to leave.

He'd still wanted to kiss her.

Which made him a fool.

Unfortunately, it seemed to be in his DNA that when he fell for someone, that was it. Because he'd never been able to find another woman who rested perfectly in the contours of his heart, the way Cora had. No one even came close.

He'd never had the desire to go hunting, either. His heart had already found the one it wanted and nothing had been able to convince it to look at anyone else.

So he hadn't.

He'd pushed the crooked gate out of the way and stepped into the yard, under the big, winter-bare oak tree, when a woman, carrying a girl with long legs sticking out of a dress and skinny arms wrapped tightly around the woman's neck, came to the doorway.

The woman's long brown hair hung haphazardly out of her lopsided bun. She wore a loose skirt that fell the whole way to her toes, which were bare, pink, and sticking out.

He couldn't see much of her body, because the girl was really too big to be carried, but her face was a familiar heart shape.

His heart tripped.

Then she looked at him.

Deep, soulful brown eyes that were dark, maybe even black—they changed according to her mood—and he'd recognize them anywhere. They haunted his dreams quite often.

Sometimes he hated them.

Sometimes they were closing as he bent to kiss her. Finally.

Currently they widened in surprise, and he thought she recognized him. But he realized it was just because an unexpected visitor stood in her yard.

He wished he had his cowboy hat instead of the ball cap, although the ball cap fit in much better here in the east and traveled better on his bike. He wouldn't feel so exposed. But he wanted her to recognize him, didn't want to have to introduce or explain himself. Not to her.

So he stood, waiting. His hands at his sides and his riding boots planted. He wore simple blue jeans and a button-down. Maybe he was a little taller, a little broader. The stubble on his face wasn't there when he left.

"Oh, dear God," Cora breathed. The little girl started to slip down her front. She cried, and Cora tightened her grip, although it looked like she swayed a little. Her skirt wavered. "Abner?" Her voice was barely a whisper.

Shock? Or fear? He wasn't sure.

He wanted to go to her, take the child from her arms, and put his own around her. Give her his strength.

At the same time, anger bubbled up in his chest, hot and thick.

He didn't move. He wasn't setting foot in that house if it was Cora's.

"My mother live here?" he asked, trying to keep his voice level. Emotionless.

"Yep." A trace of the old Cora surfaced. She'd be in bare feet. Casual. Friendly. It had changed sometime in the year before he left.

"She own the place?" he asked, still not wanting to walk in if Cora's husband was the responsible person.

"She sends the rent check out. Guess that makes it hers." Cora had recovered. She was always quick.

Too quick.

He figured the girl she was holding must be hers, too. And now there was a little one toddling out, tugging on her skirt. That one had dark hair and sparkling brown eyes. Like her mother.

His jaw had clenched so tight against the undulations in his chest, his teeth squeaked and his jaw muscles ticked in and out.

"You can send her out." His eyes felt hot and his face stiff, but his voice was still level.

Her lips tightened. Another little one, this one a boy, bigger than the child already holding her skirt but smaller than the one she carried, grabbed a hold of her. She managed to keep the bigger child in her arms while a hand came down, touching the heads of the two that were clutching her skirts. Soothing.

She shook her head. "You'd better come in."

His feet itched to turn and leave. The family he'd always wanted was right here in this house, but it belonged to another man.

The hate and bitterness that had lodged in his heart for so long erupted from his mouth when it opened. "Can I come in without being accused of being the father of your next child?"

Old memories, a jolt of guilt, and a flash of pain passed across her face in the milliseconds before her eyes narrowed and the hate he wanted to see there appeared. "Don't touch me. Don't touch my kids. You can come in, speak to your mother, then scram like the rodent you are."

She spun, maybe intending to disappear back inside the house, maybe she was running from him—a good idea—but her hasty retreat was spoiled, because the little one holding onto her skirt fell as Cora twisted. The other one, slightly more steady on his feet, didn't fall but was off-balance enough to crack his head on the corner of the door-frame. Both children started screaming.

As did the one she was holding as she tried to bend and pick up the smaller of the two from off the floor.

If it had been anyone else, anyone else in the world, he would have stridden over immediately and helped them. Happily. He had a knack with little kids, and they seemed to like him. Maybe it had been his unconventional upbringing: Amish for thirteen years, surrounded by small children, then plucked out of that life and jerked down into a life of rigid schoolrooms with only his own grade, which was full of kids who didn't understand him, were far less mature in some ways and far more mature in others, wore different clothes, different hair, different accents, and were quick to make fun of their differences.

He'd longed for his old comfortable Amish home and the happiness of the children around him, even if his father was severe and his Amish stepmother hated him.

Cora barely kept from dropping the toddler on the step as she struggled to get a hold on her while keeping her balance as the older child clung to her neck. The cries of all three kids grew louder. From in the house, someone shouted.

Frig it.

Abner was up the steps and picking up the screaming toddler before he gave it another thought. It didn't hurt kids to cry. They needed to sometimes. But hopefully, he'd never be such a jerk that he'd enjoy watching unnecessary suffering.

While Cora was adjusting the bigger girl in her arms, he scooped the little boy up as well. Now they could cry because a stranger was holding them, rather than because their mother wasn't.

He'd just better not run into her husband sitting inside with his feet propped up, beer can in one hand and TV remote in the other. He'd seen it a lot growing up in the English world, although his mother had never been married to any of those losers. They'd come and gone slightly more often than he'd gotten a new pair of shoes.

If Cora's husband was like that... Abner's fingers itched to ball up. That could be ugly.

See? He wasn't a violent man. Didn't even have a temper. Yet, he'd been in Cora's presence for less than five minutes, and already he itched to throttle someone. She brought out those deeper emotions in him, and he always wanted to either grab her or kiss her...but not now. He didn't want to kiss her. He didn't even know her. She'd changed. He'd changed.

"Put the kids down!" she shouted over the crying of the little ones. He thought he'd heard a door slam somewhere, too.

Despite the wiggling kid in each arm, he lifted a brow at her, then, deliberately, he turned his back, still holding the children, and walked down the dark hall, looking for a room to set them in.

Yeah, she stirred him all right, and they might be her kids, but she didn't get the privilege of bossing him around.

The boys from outside came racing into the hall. They skidded to a stop when they saw him. He paused while their eyes went from the top of his ball cap to his driving boots and back to their siblings, or half-siblings, that he held in his arms.

Normally, he had a grin and a smile and a joke that loosened kids' natural reserve and got them to trust him. Even if the babies in his arms weren't still crying loudly, he wouldn't have gotten his mouth to work.

Both of those boys had Cora's stamp all over them. Dark hair, those brown eyes with the twinkle he remembered, and her pointed chin, the lines smoothed a little on their more masculine head shape but definitely Cora's.

If he had to guess, he'd say they had different fathers.

Neither of which was him.

He body-slammed that thought and ripped his eyes away.

Beyond the boys was what looked to be a small kitchen. A step ahead to his left, there was a doorway. He could see a TV flashing.

He aimed toward the room with the TV, assuming there'd be a sofa or something he could throw the kids on.

Cora yelled something behind him, maybe telling him to put the kids down, but he ignored her and stepped into the living room.

The TV blared over the crying of the kids. Abner glanced at the screen—one man in formal clothes surrounded by a bunch of women in fancy dresses. He turned away.

A woman sat on the deflated couch. Graying hair and glasses, wearing a large blue t-shirt and leggings, slippers on her feet. Her hand sat on the coffee table, clutched around a glass of amber liquid.

A baby girl, younger than any of the other children, sat cuddled up next to the lady, holding a teething ring. She looked up, with Cora's brown eyes, as they walked in. Her brows crinkled, and she seemed to press closer to the woman beside her.

He didn't recognize the woman until her head came up. Her eyes were a little bloodshot and slightly rheumy, her face held more wrinkles, and her figure was matronly rather than curvy, but it was definitely his mother.

It felt like she'd aged fifty years, rather than almost ten.

No recognition entered her eyes.

The TV continued to blast, the kids kept crying, and at some point, a mixed-breed dog had started running laps around the living room, barking.

Cora started yelling something, and so help him, if she told him to put the kids down one more time, he'd stay and hold them all day just to spite her.

The little girl on the couch made six kids.

He'd guess at least three different dads, but he could see Cora on each face, and his heart bled.

At least her current man must be working. Abner hadn't seen him yet, anyway.

Someone muted the TV. Abner set the two kids he carried down on the couch.

His mother followed his movements with her eyes but still didn't seem to know who he was. It was his fault for staying away so long, but that didn't change the fact that his chest pinched, and he wished Cora would leave the room because he had a feeling he was going to have to introduce himself to his mother, which probably shouldn't surprise him since she'd given him away at birth and hardly seemed to want him when he'd been sent back at thirteen after his dad had been killed in the accident that was Abner's fault.

His Amish stepmother might have kept him, except the son she'd had at the same time Abner's mother had had him was killed in that same accident. How could she not look at Abner and think he should have been the one to die?

So, he'd gone to live with his mother and his half-brother, Doug, and her current squeeze—Abner couldn't even remember his name. He'd been gone in less than a year anyway.

He'd gone from being out of school and working a man's job and a man's hours to being considered a kid again and placed in a classroom where he was the butt of every joke.

It was funny that Cora was here now, with his mother. There was a connection there, but it wasn't strong.

"Jacob?" his mom rasped, her fingers tightening around her drink.

That was his dad. Abner understood the confusion, made worse by the drink, probably. He looked at a shadow of his father in the mirror every morning.

Acutely aware of Cora behind him, and not wanting anything from her, least of all her pity, he willed himself not to fidget.

"It's Abner, Mom."

Her eyes didn't flicker. No reaction at all. Nothing. For about five seconds.

The kids had stopped screaming, and the two boys had a hold on the dog. It was quiet enough that he could hear Cora's pity-filled exhale behind him.

He wanted to turn on her and grab her and tell her he didn't care. It didn't matter that his mother didn't know him and had never wanted him and his Amish mother had sent him away. He didn't care because he didn't have a heart and he didn't have feelings and he could bury it all and be a machine.

His desire to be back under the wide-open skies and cold winds of North Dakota almost felt like a punch in the gut. He belonged there. Felt worthy and wanted.

He still fought the urge to leave because he didn't do the easy thing, never, whatever that was.

Finally, his mother's mouth opened, and understanding seemed to dawn across her face. "Abner? You look like Jacob."

"Doug said you wanted to see me." He hadn't moved from his position in the middle of the floor, and no one else had stirred, either.

His mother held her hand—the one that wasn't gripping her drink on the coffee table—out to him.

He didn't really want to take it but felt he had little choice. He stepped forward and took her soft, plump, slightly damp hand in his.

"I'm moving to North Carolina and wanted to see you before I go."

He had to feel something for her. She was his mother.

But he wasn't sure what it was, and her words didn't cause him any undue alarm nor any deep desire to stay and bond with her. He'd thought she'd have something to say about her mother passing. About the funeral. About the years he'd been gone.

He didn't really feel like she owed him an apology. But, yeah, even that.

Actually, he felt relief, because now she'd seen him and now he could go. He didn't want to care.

Her fingers tightened. "Stay for a couple of days."

No. He couldn't. Not with Cora and her husband sleeping under the same roof.

"He can be your new boyfriend, Mommy," the oldest of the boys said.

Abner didn't mean to squeeze his mother's hand so hard, and he sure didn't want to turn and look at Cora, but he did both.

She ignored him. Of course. "No. No more boyfriends." She spoke to her son. "Take that dog back to the neighbor's house where he belongs and come right home." The boy took a hold of the collar and gave Abner one last glance before dragging it out.

Cora moved toward the couch. "Do you need anything, Aunt Sandy, before I take the kids into the kitchen and make them some sandwiches?"

Cora had been getting together with Stephen, Abner's cousin, when Abner left. Stephen would have called Abner's mother Aunt Sandy. Looked like Cora had picked it up, too.

His mother picked her drink up off the coffee table and held it in front of her mouth. "Get me a refill." She tipped the glass up and drained it, then turned her eyes to the TV.

She'd just lost her mother, and Abner could cut her some slack for that, but her behavior seemed a little...selfish.

But...before that. New boyfriend? Made it sound like there was an old boyfriend. And no husband.

Not that he cared. He could barely stand Cora.

"Come on, guys. Let's wash up, and you can help me." Cora scooped the baby off the couch and held a few fingers out for the little one who had turned over on his stomach and had her little chubby legs sliding off and onto the floor.

The girl settled on her belly hanging there, and Cora walked off without her.

She passed behind Abner, and he caught her scent. She used to smell like bubble gum and cotton candy.

Her scent had matured along with the rest of her, more deeply feminine, subtly sweet. A lighter scent, but the pull on him was stronger, harder, like he was caught in a rip current. He clenched his jaw and fisted his hand, unwilling to be dragged anywhere. Least of all by Cora.

His mother had asked him to stay. He wasn't going to. Couldn't. Not for the night.

But his mother obviously wasn't doing well. Whether that was because of the death of her mother, or if that was her current state, he didn't know.

Regardless, she obviously needed help, and Cora obviously didn't have the resources to give it to her. Physical or monetary.

His mother ignored him. Her gaze stuck on the TV that had been unmuted. The blaring noise irritated him in a way the crying, even screaming, of children didn't. Her eyes were glassy, and she seemed to have forgotten him.

He picked up the toddler that was now struggling to get off the couch and turned toward the kitchen. He didn't have anything to say to Cora, but she might be able to shed some light on the situation with his mother.

Chapter 2

It'd been years since Cora had the luxury of a few quiet moments. Her fault. She owned it. She knew exactly how kids were made, and she took responsibility for her actions.

The problem was she was a sucker for a kind word and couldn't tell the difference between a rake and a good man. "Good man" seemed like an oxymoron to her, but hey, she supposed the impossible was possible, just with someone else. Not her.

Right now, though, she'd really appreciate just a few seconds to pull herself together.

Abner.

She hated him.

Mostly.

He was a cold, egotistical jerk.

Except, back when they'd been friends and she'd hoped to use him to make his cousin jealous, she'd ended up falling for him, because underneath that tough-guy façade, she'd found he was actually sweet and soft as fluff.

She'd ruined it, of course. Or maybe she should say her brother-in-law, whom she was living with, along with her sister, at the time, had ruined it.

No. She was a big believer in taking responsibility for her own actions.

She'd taken a gamble. And she'd lost Abner. Because he'd been too much of a prideful stick-in-the-mud to see that things weren't what they seemed.

Well, she'd faced everything without him. She'd managed to survive then, and she didn't need him now. Except he'd followed her into

14

the kitchen. She didn't turn to see him. She could just tell he was there. Shivers that she didn't know she was capable of cascaded down her back and out her arms.

She didn't want him, but it wasn't her house, and she could hardly kick him out. Aunt Sandy had been kind enough to allow her to move in even though their family ties were dubious. It had been beneficial to both of them, since Cora moving in had kept Aunt Sandy from needing to move to a smaller place. But Cora was being evicted at the end of the month after Aunt Sandy left for North Carolina.

But she didn't have to talk to him. Maybe if she ignored him, he'd leave. He'd sure left fast enough all those years ago without a single thought that maybe there was more to the story than he'd heard.

"Mommy, I'm hungry." Summer still clung to her neck. Of all her kids, Summer had been the closest to "Grammy," even though Abner's grandmother wasn't theirs. She was really a great-aunt to some of her kids—Derrick and Summer, the ones that were Stephen's.

"Ungwee." Luna, who was surprisingly content in Abner's arms where he stood in the doorway, repeated Summer's complaint.

With her foot, Cora grabbed a wobbly chair leg and pulled. It came out from the table with a scraping sound. She adjusted Summer's body so her feet planted on the chair. The five-year-old squeezed tighter with her arms, and Cora spent a few moments reassuring her that she would hold her once again as soon as everyone else had food.

Her back sighed in acute relief as Summer settled in the chair. Ignoring the tall man standing just feet away holding her toddler, Cora settled Claire, her youngest, in her highchair and slid her closer to the table, setting a cracker down in front of her to keep her from getting out.

Abner had spent his primary years with the Amish, and it shouldn't be a surprise to her that he was good with children. She just wasn't used to men like that. It was just one more thing that added to everything she remembered that made him appealing. A feeling she needed to fight. Her feelings had never been reliable.

Andrew, her oldest, already had the bread out as Derrick burst back in the door after taking the dog home. "Derrick, go into the room and find the babies' sippy cups."

Derrick turned to do as he'd been told, and Cora turned to the refrigerator, glad it was placed in such a position that her back was to Abner.

Why didn't he just leave?

She didn't even try to tell him to put her child down. He'd not listened to her the last three times she'd told him, and something told her he wasn't going to start listening to her now.

Grabbing the meat tray that the church had provided to the family, she set it on the small counter and started piling meat onto the slices of bread Andrew had set out. She didn't know why she bothered; the kids were just going to take them apart. Some of them would eat the bread, some the meat, and they'd all lick the mayonnaise clean off everything. Andrew was putting it on liberally. She told herself it was made out of egg whites and was probably healthy in some way for them. And someday when she didn't feel like she was walking around in a fog with a child clinging to her for all her waking hours, she might actually have vegetables to go with them too.

Oh, yeah. She needed money for vegetables. Especially this time of year. Her design business might provide that eventually.

Not now.

She turned with the sandwiches. Abner had put Luna in her booster seat, given Claire another cracker, and was helping Kohlton give everyone a napkin and a drink.

Fury burned hot up her neck. She could have used his help once upon a time, but not now.

"No one invited you in here." She hated the anger in her voice, and she hated even more the awful example she was being for her children.

Everyone was always welcome in this house. "If you need to stay, go talk to your mother and let me alone."

He ignored her, taking three cups of water from the sink and putting them in front of the older three kids' places.

He was a jerk, but he wasn't dangerous. She opened the cupboard door—gingerly, because it was only attached by one crooked hinge, the one she and Andrew had put on—grabbed the bottle of alcohol, and stomped toward the doorway, intending to refill Aunt Sandy's glass.

She turned and was only able to take one step before she had to stop. Or run into Abner.

She wasn't touching him.

"Excuse me. Your mother needs a refill." She kept her face impassive and stared at the button on his shirt.

"No."

Whether he was telling her no, that he wasn't excusing her or no, she didn't need a refill, Cora wasn't sure and didn't care.

"Fine. You take it in." She held the bottle up between them, still not looking at him.

"No."

"Mommy, I'm hungry."

"Can we eat?"

"Hungwee."

One of her kids started pounding on the table. The others joined in.

Still, Abner didn't move.

Fed up with his silent judgment and his intimidation tactics, Cora gritted her teeth and spun. "Summer, ask the blessing. Derrick, give Claire another cracker." She barked out orders—called out loudly to be heard over the pounding—which was the only way she'd found to deal with six little ones at once. Become a drill sergeant.

She certainly hadn't had any examples of good parenting growing up. Her dad had left before she could remember and she could pass him on the street tomorrow and she wouldn't know him.

It was a wonder she hadn't ended up in foster care with the casual way her mom dropped her off on whoever was willing to take her, sometimes for weeks and months at a time.

A couple of times she'd stabilized and had a man around. On one of those occasions, Cora had become friends with her new step-sister Erin. Erin had ended up marrying Abner's half-brother, Jason, and Cora had lived with them for a while.

She hadn't wanted to become like her mother. Her deepest desire was to provide a more stable homelife for her children. So far, she'd been a failure. But she'd chosen to turn her life around, and she was determined to do it.

She marched around the table, intending to hit the doorway from the opposite side, bypassing the man who stood in her kitchen like he belonged there.

His eyes followed her, but he didn't move. She supposed she should be grateful, but it just made her angrier. How dare he come in here and watch her like she was a bug on the wall? And judge her. Like giving a grieving woman alcohol was a sin or something.

Her conscience poked her. It wasn't like Aunt Sandy had just started drinking when her mother died. She was definitely past the parameters of an alcoholic and had been for some time. But Cora couldn't afford the rent check on her own. She needed Aunt Sandy's disability checks. They paid the rent and bought alcohol. Cora took care of everything else with the little she made in her business and child support for four of her six kids. None for Andrew. None for Kohlton.

Her fault.

She walked into the living room. Aunt Sandy didn't even look at her. Cora filled the glass to the top.

She'd gotten swept into alcohol abuse for a few years. It had done nothing but amplify her bad decisions. It was great for numbing pain, and honestly, it was a temptation now, but she'd never done a single smart thing while under the influence. And she'd determined, for her children, she was going to be smart from now on.

So, she'd put the lid back on the bottle of seduction and carried it out of the room.

She'd been gone all of ninety seconds. Seriously.

She could hardly believe the vision that greeted her in her kitchen. Her children were sitting quietly at the table, Abner holding Luna on his lap, and they were all eating their sandwiches. Crusts first.

"Hey, Mom! Look at us!" Derrick called out. He bit off another bite of his crust. One entire side of crust was gone, and he was half done with a second side.

"Eating crust puts hair on your chest," Summer sang out happily, munching on another bite of her own crust.

Cora's brows went up. "I guess we won't have to worry about you getting married young."

"Huh?" Summer said, with her mouth full.

"Don't talk with your mouth full," Cora said, biting off any other sarcastic comments that Abner seemed to have brought out in her. If Summer was going to eat her crust, Cora would be a fool to ruin it by explaining that chest hair wasn't exactly an asset to a female. Maybe it would keep her from turning out like Cora had.

No. Chest hair wouldn't have prevented Andrew.

She steeled herself and looked at Abner, hating that he seemed to have six small children completely under control. The perfect man. Who, of course, wanted a perfect woman. Even back when she was eighteen, she was too messed up for him.

His eyes, which had held humor as he looked at her children, became serious, unreadable, when they turned her way. She returned his stare.

He stood, looking back over the kids. "I'll have your mom check your chests for hair at bath time tonight."

"Aww, you're not leaving?" Derrick whined.

Luna gripped his neck, her half sandwich clutched in one fist.

He strode to her and held Luna out. Normally, Luna cried when anyone but Cora held her, but she leaned her body to Abner and didn't reach out for her mother.

"I wanna talk to you," he said.

That was just great. Luna finally found a man that didn't make her scream, and it had to be Abner, of all people. At least maybe she'd grow up to have good taste in men. Better than Cora, although Abner had always been her first choice. Even when she hated him, she could admit he was a good man. He just didn't want her.

"Then talk."

"I don't think you want to have this conversation in front of your children."

She wanted to lip off. Say something smart. Let him know that she wasn't catering to him and he'd have the conversation at her convenience.

But the look in his eye said he'd have it now if she insisted, and she'd made the decision to put her kids first. So, as much as she wanted to put him in his place, she grabbed Luna from him. "I normally have them in bed by nine."

It was eight, actually. But she didn't have very many things in her favor, and she could give herself the advantage of cleanliness if she had time to shower first. It would be a confidence booster. One didn't face their adversary at any more of a disadvantage than absolutely necessary.

"I'll be back at nine."

"You're not staying here."

His brows twitched. "I am."

Her breath huffed out in frustration. With him and with herself. She was pretty sure he hadn't been planning on staying until she said something. If she could have just kept her big mouth shut.

Chapter 3

The pain in Abner's chest hadn't eased at all. Not with a trip to the hardware store. Not as he'd walked the sidewalks and the few friendly people out and about had smiled and nodded as they passed. Not as he sat in the cool, dark sanctuary of the little church where he'd parked his bike.

The sky was clear, and there'd be a frost but no rain. He'd leave the bike at the church. It was his one vanity. If one could call it that. It was an antique. And he'd restored it to mint condition. It was uncomfortable as heck to ride but looked cool. He was no stranger to being uncomfortable.

Although his discomfort had reached a level even he wasn't used to today in Cora's kitchen. His mother might pay the rent, but Cora was the responsible adult in that house.

There'd been a car at the house earlier when he'd gone by. Maybe mourners or well-wishers.

It was gone now, though, as he walked through the silent, dark town toward Cora's house. It'd been a quiet town. A couple of elderly people on porches, a few cars, especially a little after three when the shift at the coal mine let out, and a few kids running on the sidewalks. The hardware store had been mostly deserted.

The Amish community he'd grown up in was only ten or fifteen miles away, but Abner had no desire to go back. They wouldn't shun him—he'd never joined the church—but he didn't fit in there anymore.

He'd have been happy being Amish.

Except for Cora.

He strode up the walk, shifting the bags of supplies he carried to one hand, and knocked on the door.

She kept him waiting. Of course.

He wanted to hold on to his hatred. His feelings of deep betrayal. His hurt and anger. But he couldn't when he had six sets of Cora's eyes looking at him.

He wasn't even sure he could do it when only Cora was looking at him.

The door opened.

She had a sweater on. Jeans. Still in her bare feet. Despite the cold, she stepped out, closing the door behind her.

It made him angry. He'd planned to stay somewhere else. Hadn't really thought he'd sleep in the house with Cora and her kids, even if it was his mother's and she wanted him to stay.

But he felt like she was trying to outmaneuver him by closing the door and not inviting him in.

He caught her scent as she slipped by him. Mixed with the cool air and the night darkness, it was far more lethal than it had been earlier in the house under the harsh lights with her children running around.

He should have held his breath.

She crossed her arms over her chest and leaned against the porch post, looking out at the quiet street.

She didn't look at him when she spoke. "What did you want?"

He pushed the anger aside. "Maybe we can act like adults here."

"I am."

"I meant I'll pretend you didn't cheat on me, stab me in the back, and lie about me to our friends, family, and the whole town, if you can manage to be civil."

Her jaw jutted out. "That's the way you're civil and 'act like an adult?' By throwing up everything I've ever done and rubbing my face in it? Or you just want to make sure I know where I stand, and it's well below you." There was tension in every line of her body. "I know it, Abner. If you only came here to tell me what an idiot I am, you can stop wasting your breath."

Why did he do that?

He knew. Because keeping his mouth shut wasn't something he normally had a problem with. Nor was being nice. And the Amish took pride in their humility. Ha. A contradiction, sure, but true nonetheless. It'd been beaten into him from a young age.

He hadn't learned the lesson as well as he thought.

So, he'd do the hard thing.

Oh, but it grated. Because she'd never apologized to him.

"I'm sorry. You're right. Those were fighting words."

Her head snapped around at his apology. Too bad he couldn't get the expression on his face to match his words.

Yeah, she saw the anger. Her eyes narrowed.

"Forgiven," she said with a slight tilt of her head that said plain as an interstate billboard that she was totally adding his fake apology to his list of faults.

Which made him even angrier. She was the one with the long list of faults. He'd been clear about his intentions.

He swallowed his anger. Again.

"What's up with my mom?"

"She's an alcoholic. She's not interested in treatment, and I believe until she wants to quit, there's no point in me fighting her about it." Cora stared straight ahead, her arms crossed like a shield, her words as clipped as her twang would allow.

"So you just let her sit on the couch and be drunk all day?"

"I let her?" Cora turned on him. "Me? This is my fault?" Her eyes widened, and she huffed out a breath. "Where have you been the last nine years? Out being the morally righteous ringleader far away from anyone who would consider you family? Now all the sudden, you give a crap?" She shook her head but didn't pause long enough to give him a chance to respond. "That's rich. You've ignored her for nine years, and it's my fault she's an alcoholic." She spun. "I'm sorry. I can't have a rational conversation with someone who can't take responsibility for his actions and casts blame wherever there's a convenient body."

She strode to the door, her hand out for the knob.

He couldn't touch her. He'd end up strangling her. Or worse, kissing her.

"I didn't mean it like that, and you know it. You're just taking it as wrong as you can because you have some crazy bug up your butt that probably has to do with guilt and the female tendency to convolute logic until it's unrecognizable as anything but bs."

If she wanted to leave, he wasn't stopping her. He wasn't getting any useful information out of her anyway. He'd go to the viewing tomorrow night and the funeral the next day then blow the joint.

His mother had never given a crap about him. Why should he care about her now?

But it didn't matter. He did and he would and all the other stupid things his conscience wouldn't let him out of.

"Well, with that chauvinistic attitude toward women, it's no wonder you're not married."

"How do you know the frig I'm not?" he spat out, more angry than he could remember being since the last time he saw Cora.

"Oh, I suppose you are the kind of man who would leave his wife at home while he went to his grandmother's funeral and take his wedding ring off while he was doing it. Classy." Her eyes snapped, but there was a vulnerability to her that could melt his anger away, if he'd let it. He couldn't.

"Classy?" She was accusing him of not being classy? Seriously? "I guess I'm just not up with the times where having six kids to three different men is the new classy."

"Shut up, jerk." She shoved the door open. Either she was almost as angry as he was, or she lost her grip on the doorknob, because it slammed against the wall with a crack and thud. Guess he should have bought a doorstop at the hardware store, too.

He was so furious his hands shook, rattling the plastic bags he held, but he wasn't so angry he missed his opportunity.

Stepping into the house while she was still fumbling for the door in the dark, he walked past her, through the pitch-black hall, and into the kitchen. As he passed the entrance to the living room, the TV screen blinked, but it was muted. It looked like his mother had passed out on the couch. He could hear her uneven snores as he walked by.

"I am not going to allow you to sleep in this house," Cora hissed in a whisper behind him.

"That's fine. I'm not asking for your permission."

"I'll call the police."

He laughed. "Really? I'm the son of the owner. They're more likely to throw you out." He almost added another, worse insult, but he bit it back. "I don't know what the problem is anyway. We both know I never touched you. Not tempted to now, either."

Lie. It was such a lie.

He'd always had a good poker face, but it was fortunate he had his back to her. A lie that big, she'd have to know it.

"Right. We already established that you're perfect and I'm not. You can keep rubbing it in, but no one's listening." Her voice had softened. Not sure what that meant. But it made him a little sad. She'd obviously had some hard knocks, but she hadn't quit fighting. He could admire that.

He set two of the bags he carried on the table. "You'll want to do something with these before they spoil."

He wasn't tired, and he had a few things he wanted to do with the stuff in the other bags, but he figured he needed to stake his claim.

"You can sleep in the recliner, and I'll take your bed, or I'll sleep in the recliner. Your choice." He walked to the hall doorway and paused, his back to her. Waiting for her to tell him to sleep in the recliner.

Finally, she said softly, "Your mother's room is the door on the right at the top of the steps. Claire is in there in a play yard. The rest of the children sleep in the other room. The recliner is where I always sleep."

Something tightened in his chest. He didn't want to feel it, and he steeled himself against it. "I'll sleep in the recliner."

Another drawn-out silence like she was weighing her words.

"There's a pillow and blanket folded up behind it," she said begrudgingly.

He turned.

She held up her hand. "Don't. Whatever you're going to say, don't. You're here because I can't throw you out. That's the only reason. And I'm staying because I can't leave my children. There's no need for us to talk to each other."

His brow twitched at that. "So, we're not fighting now; you're just giving me the silent treatment?"

Her lips flattened and pulled back, but she didn't say anything.

"Thought that was something that only happened to married men. How did I get so lucky?"

"Maybe, it's you," Cora suggested in a fake-helpful way.

"Do I get a point every time you talk? Maybe a point for each word? If so, I'm up by three."

He had to turn and walk out of the kitchen. Otherwise, he was going to laugh at her balled hands and red face.

Chapter 4

After a restless night, Cora came down the stairs early the next morning, Claire in her arms and Luna holding on to one hand.

It was Friday, but she wasn't going to make her older children go to school. They hadn't gone for the last two days. Not since the woman they called Grammy had passed of an apparent heart attack. Aunt Sandy wasn't much of an adult figure in their lives, but Grammy, her mother, had been like a grandmother. The kids had taken it hard. Like children, they were fine one minute, playing and fighting, and the next, they were all crying and trying to pile in her lap.

Next week was Thanksgiving, and they'd have the holiday and extra time off for hunting season to catch up on their school.

Although Aunt Sandy had said she planned on leaving at the end of the month. That had been before her mother died. Grammy had told Cora not to worry, that they'd figure out a place for her to go.

Cora didn't really believe Aunt Sandy anyway. Pretty much every month last year from November to March, Aunt Sandy said she was moving someplace warmer. It hadn't happened. Cora had stopped worrying about it.

As she hit the last step, she realized that she'd been smelling coffee for a while. Had to be Abner. Aunt Sandy wouldn't be up for hours.

After looking in the living room and seeing her aunt lying on the couch on her stomach, her hand still gripping the neck of an empty bottle, Cora decided she might not be up at all. She hoped Aunt Sandy was sober enough to go to the viewing tonight.

That was a long time away. She had a whole day to get through and a man to deal with, and she'd not gotten much sleep. She had another two, maybe three hours before her current project of designing a website for a garbage-hauling company in New Hampshire was complete. Hopefully tonight. Then it had to be approved before she received the other half of her pay. It wouldn't be enough for a security deposit and a first month's rent, but maybe she'd find a place that would forgo the deposit.

She'd think about that later, too, she decided as she stepped into the kitchen. Abner stood at the counter, cracking eggs into a bowl. Brown eggs. Not the cheap white ones she always bought.

Last night, he'd bested her, and they both knew it. She needed all the brain she had left to try not to get as soundly beaten again today. Too bad he didn't mean it when he suggested they try to put their differences aside and act like adults.

But he thought she'd lied about him on purpose to hurt him, and he'd left her when she most needed him. How could they ever get past that?

Claire waved her hands and smiled at Abner, even though his back was to them. That was odd since Claire seldom wanted anyone but her.

Cora ignored her and helped Luna into her booster seat.

"Morning."

How could she hate him and yet his voice still caused her heart to flip?

"Hello." She couldn't bring herself to say good morning to him. Was it a good morning when the person she hated most in the world was in her kitchen?

Okay. There were a few people she disliked with more intensity than Abner. Andrew's father, for example. But not many.

Maybe if she kept telling herself that, it would become truth. There was a way Abner carried himself, a look on his face that bespoke honesty and integrity. They hadn't seen each other for a long time, but that hadn't changed. She admired it back then, and she valued it even more now, knowing how rare it was.

She carefully opened the cupboard door to grab a cracker. Then stopped short. Her eyes narrowed. She moved the cupboard door back and forth. It was the same door, but it now moved with ease. Two hinges were perfectly placed, and the one she'd nailed in had been removed.

Pursing her lips, she angled her eyes over. Abner held the spatula in his hand, watching the eggs cook.

"You fixed this."

"Thought I was getting the silent treatment?" He looked up, serious. "That's seven points for me."

"I have six kids in this house. I don't need you acting like one too."

"Oh? And it's mature to not talk to someone because you're mad at them?"

She gritted her teeth together and turned away, grabbing the crackers and telling herself she didn't care that he'd fixed the cupboard door. What did it matter if he was going to be a jerk?

He turned the eggs over easy, and her mouth watered. She normally fed the kids oatmeal for breakfast. It was cheap and fast.

But he'd brought groceries home last night when he'd come in, and he'd commanded her to put them away. She'd done it, more because she couldn't see the food going to waste than because she wanted to do anything nice for him. But she hadn't bargained on him eating his food in front of her and the children.

The toaster popped up. Cora tried to breathe through her mouth. It smelled like a real breakfast with coffee and eggs and toast and that expensive, exotic food...bacon. She hadn't had bacon in forever. When he opened the oven door, the smell of smoked meat saturated the kitchen, and she almost considered trying to be nice to him. But if he gave her a piece, she'd have to share it with her kids, and she'd end up not getting any anyway.

She tried to think about moon landings and Elvis impersonators and whether or not she had enough clean underwear for all the kids for the viewing tonight. Not about bacon. The crispness and the greasy goodness and the smoked meat flavor. How if it was cooked just right it snapped and almost melted in her mouth. Bacon and eggs. Bacon and toast. Bacon and ice cream. Bacon could even make turnips taste good.

She had Claire in the highchair and had turned to get a pot out of the bottom cupboard, shoving bacon out of her mind and hoping Abner would be done at the stove soon so she didn't have to stand beside him and cook. She didn't want to stand next to his bacon either. Didn't he know how rude it was to bring his own food into her house and cook it in front of her?

Behind her, she could hear him buttering the toast. She bit the insides of her cheeks and slipped around to put water in the pan.

A plate clanked on the table. Then a second one.

"You usually feed the baby off your plate?" he asked.

She swallowed before she started drooling—he cooked himself such a large breakfast it took two plates?

"Yes," she said, without even really thinking.

"Can Luna feed herself?"

She shut the water off and turned. What in the world?

"That's for Luna?"

"Yeah. Can she eat some bacon if I break it into small pieces?"

She put the water on the stove. "Yes, she can feed herself, and yes, she can have small pieces of bacon."

"That plate's for you. Eat it while it's hot. How soon 'til the rest of the kids come down?"

He'd made her a plate. Full of all the things he was cooking. The eggs had been for her. There was buttered toast. And bacon. Two pieces.

Her heart warmed, and she stiffened. No. She couldn't let herself soften toward him. She'd fallen for him once, and he'd believed the worst of her and left without a word. Not happening again.

But she could be polite. For bacon.

"Thanks." She set the pan of water on the stove without turning it on and moved to the table, sitting down beside Claire's highchair and looking at the plate heaped in front of her. "I wasn't going to make the other kids go to school today. But if you're cooking breakfast, I can go get them up."

He poured more eggs into the skillet, and they sizzled. "No, don't do that. I'll eat these, then we'll cook more when they come down." He shook the skillet a little and looked over his shoulder. "Those groceries were for you."

She looked down at her plate, guilty. Why did he have to be nice? How was she supposed to keep hating him when he cooked for her and fed her children?

Without looking up, she said, "Thank you."

He set a plate on the table and sat down across from her. "I'm sorry. Truly. Maybe we can't be friends, but we can at least set a good example for your kids."

There he went again, making her feel bad. Only he didn't know it this time. What kind of example had she been for her kids? Especially the three oldest ones. She was a mess.

Was. In her past. She'd decided to do better, and she was working toward that. Working toward being a better mother, being more patient, and putting her children first. Resisting the lure of strong arms that would make her feel good for a night. Ignoring alcohol's siren call. Working on her design business. And, lastly, not falling for a man like Abner who would never get over the past.

"Thank you," she said, taking Claire's little hand in hers. "Would you say the blessing for us?" There. It wasn't hard to be nice. She forced her lips to tilt up.

Abner stared at her. "No," he finally said.

Her eyes widened. Questions swirled through her head, because she was sure, she remembered distinctly, that Abner had been a churched man. His actions, his speech, the stand he took. She remembered it clearly.

"I do, Mommy," Luna said.

"Sure, baby, you pray for us," Cora said, bowing her head and closing her eyes. Knowing her children would do what she did, even though Claire was too young to be told.

Luna mumbled words that were unclear except for the "amen" at the end.

Cora repeated the word and lifted her head, composed. Abner had bowed his head, but he hadn't repeated the "amen" and didn't look at her as he picked up a piece of Luna's bacon and started crumbling it.

"Thank you for fixing the cupboard," Cora said as she fed Claire a bite of egg.

"I'm gonna tackle that hole in the wall soon as we're done here." He put a few pieces of bacon on Luna's plate before using his fork to cut up her egg.

He was such a natural with children that she had to ask. "Do you have children?"

"No." He didn't look up.

The silence between them felt awkward as she gave Claire one more bite of egg and picked up a piece of bacon. It was too pricy, and she never bought it. She was going to enjoy it.

"Would you tell me about my mom?" he asked. Several beats passed before he said, "Please."

He sounded humble. She tilted her head at him. Looked it too. "About her drinking?"

"Yeah. Is this normal? Is she just mourning her mother?" He blew out a breath and looked across the room. "I want to fix it. I feel like I can't leave with my mother passed out drunk on the couch every day."

Cora waited until he looked back over at her. She wanted him to know she was being sincere. "It's been worse the last few days. She doesn't usually drink the hard liquor. But there are four cases of beer on the back porch, and she cracks a can at breakfast."

He jerked his chin up without saying anything.

"I would call her a functional alcoholic. You can't really tell she's buzzed all day." Cora looked down at her plate and drew her bacon through the glistening yellow of her broken yolk. "But that's what she spends her money on. Rent and beer."

"Where are you at in this?" His face was impassive, serious.

She lifted her chin. She wasn't sure what his question was for, but she didn't owe him her life history. "I make sure my kids stay out of it."

"You?" he asked again.

Derrick appeared in the doorway. "Is he your new boyfriend, Mom?"

Cora steeled herself. It was too early in the morning for her to deal with questions like that, even if it did keep her from having to answer Abner's inquiry. Plus, she wanted to savor her bacon in peace.

After one last glance that promised he wasn't done with her, he rolled with the interruption. "I've been hearing a lot about this boyfriend job. What, exactly, does it entail? I might not want it."

Cora pressed her lips together and focused on feeding the baby.

Derrick's lips turned up, and he looked at Abner with renewed interest. "It's not hard. You just sit in front of the TV and act like a jerk."

Abner stood. "Doesn't sound like a job I'm interested in."

Cora bit the insides of her cheeks while her heart hurt. Did she do such an awful job of picking men?

She knew she had. But she'd changed. She didn't need a man. Didn't want one, either. They only ended up making things worse.

The baby was content, and Cora lifted a piece of bacon, perfectly crisp and with just the right whiff of honey and smoke, glistening with golden egg yolk on the end.

"Is that bacon?" Derrick asked, stepping close, his eyes running the length of the piece of meat in her fingers.

Her mouth had been producing saliva at flood stage. She swallowed and handed the piece across the table to Derrick without saying anything.

He eyed the other piece on her plate. She kept a piece of bread for Claire and pushed the plate across the table.

"Sit and eat," she said, not even watching as he put the bacon in his mouth and pulled a chair.

She didn't look at Abner, either, as he walked to the stove.

"Are your siblings up?" he asked Derrick.

"Andrew and Summer are both coming down. They were fighting over who got the bathroom first."

"Thought I heard some scuffling up there," Abner said casually, like kids fighting was an everyday occurrence for him.

But it couldn't be, since he'd said that he didn't have any kids.

"If you stay, are you going to cook us breakfast every morning?" Derrick asked around the partially chewed eggs and bacon in his mouth.

"Don't talk with your mouth full," Cora said automatically. It was a phrase she uttered at least fifteen times a day. Once per child per meal. Claire wasn't old enough to be told.

Derrick closed his mouth, but he didn't stop staring at Abner's back.

Cora could hear something sizzling. Maybe he was cooking more eggs. She didn't look.

"I'm not staying."

She knew he wasn't. Maybe none of them were. If Aunt Sandy finally did what she claimed to be doing, they were all going to find a new place to live. She didn't burden Derrick with that knowledge.

She also didn't close her eyes and allow the odd curl of Abner's words to soak through her. He'd always had that different note to his speech, probably from growing up with the Amish. Whatever it was, it was all his, and she'd loved it back in the day.

Not anymore, of course.

He set a plate down in front of her. Same as the one before. Eggs and toast and bacon. Steaming.

She swallowed and inhaled.

Old Cora would have invited him to move in on the spot. Even if she hated him, a man who cooked breakfast was a keeper in her book.

But new Cora was pickier. She didn't fall for a man just because he did one thing right. And his eggs over easy looked exactly right. Almost as right as the bacon smelled.

She cut off a piece of the egg white, and Claire opened her mouth for it.

Andrew appeared in the doorway. "Smells good."

He'd always been a little quieter.

He looked around the kitchen. "Is this your new boyfriend, Mom?"

Cora clenched her jaw. Her kids didn't mean to embarrass her. They were only speaking from experience. They didn't know she was determined to change.

She forced a smile that felt more like wolf teeth and said, as casually as she could, "Nope."

Andrew moved to the table. "Is that bacon?"

She pushed her plate across, watching the golden crispy pieces move away from her. She should have shoved them in her mouth as soon as Abner set the plate down.

"Sit and eat." She broke off another piece of toast for Claire.

Summer appeared in the doorway as Abner set another plate down in front of her. He paused this time and seemed to watch as Summer rubbed her eyes, her blanket trailing on the ground but the corner held firmly in her left hand.

"Come here, sweetie. Hop up in your chair." She didn't even look at the bacon as she passed her plate over.

Abner was going to run out soon.

He might as well make a plate for Kohlton because she could hear the steps creaking and little thumps as he jumped from one down to the next.

Abner didn't even bother setting the next plate in front of her.

"Get up here and eat your breakfast, kiddo," he said.

Kohlton's sleepy eyes widened, going from Abner to Cora, who nodded.

"Does he live here now?" Kohlton asked as he climbed up on his chair.

"No," Cora said firmly. She wasn't getting her kids' hopes up. He might stay a few days, for the funeral and his mother, but he was leaving.

Maybe her "no" was a little more bitter than it needed to be. She'd had at least eight pieces of bacon sitting in front of her, and she'd given them all away. No normal person would be happy about that, except it had been for her children, who were all happily eating. A sacrifice that was worth it.

A plate clanked down beside her. It had golden yellow scrambled eggs on it.

"Those are for the baby."

Another plate settled directly in front of her. "This is yours, and no one else eats any of it."

Two eggs and four pieces of bacon along with toast. Cora wanted to cry. Not one of the men she'd had here over the years had cooked breakfast. None.

None had given a flip about kids that weren't theirs, which had been the reason several of them had been kicked to the curb.

And Abner was the only one who'd not only cooked but made sure she ate. And bought bacon.

He sat down again in front of the plate he'd left when the kids started straggling in, stepping over Sporty, the neighbor's dog who had wormed his way into the house. Again.

Abner's food had to be cold, but he picked up where he'd left off, the chatter of the kids not seeming to bother him.

She wished he'd leave. It was hard to hold on to her hate when he was fixing stuff and feeding her kids and her.

But she needed to keep a hold of it. If she didn't, she'd forget her resolution of more than a year ago, after Luna's and Claire's father had left. Luna had been two months old. And Cora, not even knowing she'd been pregnant with Claire, had resolved, no more. No more men.

"Where's your car?" Andrew asked.

"Drove my bike," Abner answered easily, like he wasn't offended that a preteen was interrogating him.

"You mean rode it," Derrick said.

Cora bit down on her crispy, perfect bacon, the smoky, salty taste exploding in her mouth, and tried to ignore the conversation. She also tried to not close her eyes while she chewed. It probably wasn't becoming, let alone normal, to have such a reaction over bacon.

"It's a motorcycle. I drove it." Abner's food was almost gone. Even the eggs, which had to have been cold.

"Where's it at?" Andrew narrowed his eyes, like he thought Abner might be lying.

"I parked it at the church. I'll move it before the viewing tonight." His head turned to Cora, and his eyes, unshadowed by a hat brim, caught her gaze. "Is that where the viewing is?"

She looked down, not wanting to have even that much contact with him. She couldn't be mean to him after he'd just cooked her entire family breakfast, but she could hug her hate tighter. He'd left her.

Suddenly, she wasn't sure she even wanted to finish the food on her plate.

"Yes."

"What time?"

"Seven to nine."

"Do we have to go?" Summer asked. Just like a little kid. She'd been the closest to Gram, but of course she didn't want to have to get dressed up and sit quietly for two hours.

"Yes."

Abner pinched his lips closed like he'd wanted to say more but wouldn't in front of the kids.

The kids argued about who would get to sit beside Cora at the viewing while Cora finished her food, not even enjoying it, ashamed of the way she'd treated him when he'd been so nice to her. No matter how good she thought her reasoning was, it wasn't right to act the way she had.

Eventually, she wiped faces and fingers and sent the older kids up to get dressed.

She had cleared the table and was wiping Luna's face and fingers when Abner said, from the stove where he was cleaning up, "Seems like the kids are used to a parade of boyfriends coming in and out."

Anger made her arms tense and tingle. How dare he judge her? He'd left. She set Luna down before she allowed any words out from between her clenched teeth. Trying to remember that he'd been nicer to her than anyone had in a while, she was only partially successful in modulating her voice. "What I do, or have done, is none of your business."

He didn't turn around, but his hand stopped scrubbing for a few moments. It started up again, harder and faster.

But he was quiet, so she assumed he agreed with her. But she couldn't stop the guilt that tightened her throat.

"If you leave your clothes in the bathroom, I'll make sure they get washed." It was the least she could do.

"Thanks."

Something told her he was more than capable of washing his own clothes, but she was more than capable of cooking breakfast, too.

She hadn't gotten Claire out of the highchair when there was a pounding at the door.

Visitors from church, probably, at this hour in the morning. Maybe someone bringing them supper or flowers.

She left the rag on the table and wiped her wet hands against her jeans as she walked down the hall to answer the door.

Her feet would have dragged and her heart would have been a lead weight in her chest if she had known who was on the other side.

She yanked on the knob, still uncomfortable over what she was feeling for Abner but pasting what she hoped was a sweet smile on her face.

The door popped open.

Her half-sister, Erin, stood on the porch. Their children, two teen boys, stood with her. Her husband, Jason, stood behind them, his hands on a shoulder of each of his boys. He was thicker through the middle and more jowly than he'd been the last time she'd seen him. Still, looking at him was like looking at an older version of Andrew. Made sense, since he was Andrew's father.

Chapter 5

Abner's hand squeezed the rag he'd been scrubbing the stove with. Cora had waltzed out of the kitchen to answer the door, and not even the coffee still sitting in the pot could overpower the faint scent of sweet woman that drifted past his nose.

She didn't want to like him. Not any more than he wanted to like her.

He wouldn't like her, although he could admire a woman who gave up her breakfast to feed her children. He couldn't deny there was still an attraction.

He thought she felt it too. But she was fighting it as well. It kind of made him mad, because, obviously, there'd been a lot of men she hadn't fought her attraction to.

Losers.

It was almost like she was angry at him, which didn't make sense. She was the one who had lied about him.

The baby, Claire, had started fussing when Cora walked out of the kitchen, and after about two seconds she'd gotten more serious about crying. Abner left the rag on the stove and unbuckled the baby, picking her up and holding her easily in one hand while he grabbed the rag, wiped the tray, and shoved the highchair back against the wall.

Claire grabbed baby fistfuls of his cheeks and tried to gum his chin. He had to laugh when her head jerked away, obviously not expecting the prick of his two-day-old stubble. Her expression was adorably confused. So, he was grinning when he looked up to see Cora walking like she had a stick running up each leg and out her shoulder blades, leading a couple and their two boys down the hall and into the living room.

Her posture couldn't scream discomfort any louder. He looked at the couple closer out of the corner of his eye as Claire tried to put his chin in her mouth again.

He recognized Jason, his half-brother, and jerked his head.

Jason's footstep stumbled, and he glanced around at his family before breaking ranks and going to the kitchen rather than the living room where his aunt was. "Abner?"

"Yeah."

"You're the new boyfriend?"

Man, he'd thought the kids were being kids when they'd asked him that. It had made his heart squeeze every time. Now Jason. The squeeze was harder with him.

"No."

"Thought maybe you came back to claim your kid." He grinned and laughed like it was a joke.

Abner's chest tightened, but he didn't allow a single emotion to cross his face.

Jason's smile didn't fade. "So, you're just back for Gram's funeral?"

Doug, Abner's brother, had been the one to call. Jason hadn't made the effort. Abner wouldn't hold that against him, but he wasn't laughing with the man, either. Not about Cora.

"Coffee?" Abner asked.

Jason nodded. "I haven't been back much. Too cold up here."

Jason fidgeted, running his hand over the back of a chair and shifting his weight, unable to make his eyes stop twitching around the kitchen, which, of course, made Abner wonder why. Especially since Cora had a big smile on her face, but her posture screamed that she wanted to be anywhere else.

With Claire in one arm, Abner poured a cup of coffee.

Jason was a few years older than him. Cora had been living with Erin, her half-sister, and Jason for the time Cora and he had been a couple. Well, for the time that Cora had used him to try to catch the eye of his cousin, Stephen.

"Are you the family that's living in North Carolina?" he asked, wondering if he could somehow bend the conversation to Cora and try to figure out why Jason was nervous and Cora miserable.

"Yeah. Moved there not long after you left." Jason took the coffee Abner offered.

"Thought Cora was living with you then? Funny she didn't move with you."

Jason jerked, and hot liquid splashed out of the cup and onto the table. "Ah, got my finger." Jason put the cup down and stuck his pointer finger in his mouth.

"Sorry about that."

"My fault."

The TV had been muted, and sounds of the kids playing and chasing each other came from the hall and living room. Abner still held Claire in his arm, and she didn't show any signs of wanting down.

"No, I've gotten clumsy in my old age."

"You're not that much older than me." Abner didn't want to allow the subject change. At the risk of being obvious, he said, "You were telling me why Cora didn't move with you."

"Oh, that's right. I guess you ran out on her and never found out. She and Stephen got married at the courthouse not long after you left. We moved later that month." Jason said it casually, like it wasn't a big deal. But there was more to the story. They both knew Cora was pregnant when Abner left. Abner knew the baby wasn't his.

Something gave him the feeling that Jason suspected that too.

One of his boys wandered into the kitchen. Abner nodded at him. "Sean?"

The kid nodded.

"Man, you've grown. You were just maybe kindergarten or a little older when I knew you."

"You remember Abner?" Jason asked Sean.

Sean scrunched up his face and shook his head. "No."

Normally, Abner would engage the kid in conversation. But right now, he was more concerned about what was going on with Jason and, more importantly, Cora.

Before Abner could figure out anything to ask, Jason took a sip of his coffee and said, "Aunt Sandy is coming back to North Carolina with us. She's got a friend who lives nearby, and she's moving in with her. I figured you were up here, gonna shack up with Cora."

Abner's neck hairs bristled at the crudeness of Jason's words and the implied insult to Cora.

"No." He finished wiping the table, Claire's hands pulling on the short hairs of his neck, reminding him he should have gotten a haircut. It hurt, but it was a pain that grounded him. "You staying here tonight?"

"Heck no. We've got a hotel in Huntingdon. There's no room here. Not with all the rug rats Cora has running around." He lowered his voice, like they were buddies or something. "She's a good-looking girl, but someone needs to tell her how babies are made." His grin was lascivious.

Abner turned without saying anything and grabbed the butter off the counter, sticking it in the fridge.

He supposed Jason was right; Cora was completely to blame for the fact that she had six children and no man. Being that he was a big proponent of personal responsibility, if he were Cora, that's what he'd say. But the men who'd fathered those children owned just as much responsibility. If any of those children were his, he'd sure as heck wouldn't have left her to raise them on her own.

But he wasn't going to get into a moral discussion with Jason. Something told him it'd be hopeless anyway.

Shutting the refrigerator door, he turned.

Cora stood in the doorway.

Maybe they'd declared a silent truce at breakfast, but from the vitriolic look on her face, he figured they were back to full-blown warfare. Hardly fair, since it'd been Jason who'd uttered that last comment.

But Abner hadn't defended her.

His silence implied tacit agreement.

It was too late now.

Their eyes met across the kitchen. His resigned. Hers narrowed and shooting poisoned darts.

"Erin walked out to your car. She said to send you out when you were done talking." Cora stepped into the kitchen and moved away from the doorway, almost like she was making sure Jason wouldn't brush her on his way out. Andrew followed her in and stood close to her side.

Jason set his coffee down on the table. "Come on, Sean."

Sean sauntered out, lanky and long, as fifteen-year-old boys had a tendency to be. Andrew looked up at him, and Sean looked over and down.

In that moment, something about the line of their noses and the curve of their cheekbones hit Abner, and his eyes snapped to Jason.

Same line. Same curve.

Jason's lascivious smile was back in place, though muted just a bit, and his head was turned, his eyes roving over Cora. She ignored him. Her gaze was focused on Abner.

There was fear in her eyes, and a pleading he couldn't ignore.

He pressed his mouth closed. Claire gave an especially hard yank on his hair, but he barely felt it.

Jason didn't know that Andrew was his son.

Andrew was the child she was pregnant with when she'd told the town it was Abner's.

Supposedly, she'd been using Abner to get Stephen to notice her, so...how did Jason fit in?

Abner's chest tightened, and tension sizzled up his backbone. How could he have carried a torch for this woman for years? How could she be the one that no one else compared to? What was he doing, standing in her kitchen, holding her kid?

He wanted to shove the baby in her arms, leave, and never, ever come back.

Because, even though there were years between the betrayal that was even worse than he'd originally thought and now, it still hurt, in a wrenching way that felt like screws being hand-turned into his heart.

The door slammed behind Jason, but Cora hadn't moved. Like she was waiting for him to say something.

Well, she could wait forever, because there wasn't anything for him to say.

Finally, she moved, her hand resting on Andrew's shoulder in a loving gesture that made Abner long for a loving mother of his own in a way he hadn't for years and years. Not since he'd stood in his Amish home after the accident that killed his father and half-brother and had the woman who'd been raising him tell him she didn't want him anymore.

She'd had her hands on two of her "real" children just like Cora did now as she spoke. The pain of losing her husband and son was in her face her heart, too, Abner knew. It'd been real. Of course.

But the pain of her words had cut his soul just as deep as the death of his father and best friend and half-brother. They'd been more like twins, partners in good works and crimes alike. Becoming the dependable men their father had wanted. His heart had been broken, shattered, because the accident had been his fault.

His stepmother had multiplied that pain.

"Andrew, take Claire from Mr. Coblantz, and we'll put coats on and go outside for a while."

Mr. Coblantz? Really?

It was her way of putting distance between them, knowing he'd just seen something that, as far as he knew, no one else knew. Still, it hit him, probably as she intended.

Claire tried to hold onto him as he handed her over to Andrew. He pulled his eyes away from Cora. He'd known it was a bad idea to come back. And even though he disliked her, maybe more now than he had before, he wanted to fix everything, ease her load, carry her burden, walk with her, holding her hand and making her laugh.

She turned and walked out of the kitchen with her head up. Something about her posture reminded him of a fact he'd forgotten: she hadn't had a mother who cared about her, either.

Chapter 6

Abner had a sponge in one hand and a small bucket of water in the other, wiping down the spackling he'd put up last night, evening it out. It was going to take another coat. It'd been years since he'd done work like this.

His father had owned a construction business, and he and his half-brothers had worked in it from a very young age. Roofs had been their specialty. Hot, dirty work that could kill a man. No one wanted to be on a black house roof in the middle of a ninety-degree summer day.

Metal roofs weren't as hot, but the pieces were slippery and sharp. Especially in the winter. Drop one of those, and it'd slice your buddy in half on the way to the ground. Or you'd slide off it.

That's why it was so profitable for the Amish. They did what no one else wanted to do. And they did it wearing black, long sleeves and long pants.

No safety harnesses.

If he could spend all day, summer and winter, putting roofs on houses, he could do pretty much anything. It was the mindset he'd grown into.

The front door opened. Abner didn't look to see if it was Cora. She'd been out then in with the little ones for an hour or so to do laundry and make sandwiches, which she took back outside. He'd eaten lunch alone, without saying anything to Cora.

He told himself he didn't care.

"Hey, Mr. Coblantz." A voice came down the hall as the door clicked closed.

Andrew. Derrick beside him.

"Call me Abner." Their mother probably wouldn't approve, but he didn't care.

Lie.

"Abner." They moved closer. "Can we watch?" Andrew seemed to be the designated speaker. "Mom's not in a very good mood, and she said we were standing on her last nerve."

Derrick spoke for the first time. "She threatened to take us back to prison. Uh. I mean, school."

Abner grunted. "Your mom has a hard job."

"I guess." Their skinny shoulders shrugged.

Maybe it was because he'd been raised Amish, with work that had to be done in order to survive. Or maybe it was because he'd never really belonged. But he'd been very aware of how hard his mother worked. He remembered looking for opportunities to do things that would help her, but maybe he just remembered his good side. Surely, she'd looked at him and wished he'd stop picking on his siblings and making them cry and just help her instead.

Probably not. His dad would have beaten his butt, and that'd have been the end of it.

Might not be the way the rest of the world was being raised, but if he hadn't had the rod of instruction applied to his seat of knowledge, he'd probably be in jail now. He'd been pretty headstrong. That application had helped him learn to funnel his stubborn and bullheaded tendencies into perseverance, determination, and steadfastness. Taken vices and turned them into virtues, for the most part.

He still had stubborn and bullheaded tendencies.

"I'll do you one better." Abner stood up from the spackling bucket he'd been sitting on and swiped the flat edge off the floor. "Hold this." He held the edge out to Andrew then pulled the lid up.

It'd have been better if Andrew had done the first layer. With one more, Abner could have been done and ready for paint. By letting Andrew do it, it would take three coats or more.

Didn't matter. He wasn't in a rush.

Derrick had the sponge and Andrew was into the spackling up to his elbows when Cora walked in with the little ones. He didn't have to look to know it was her. He could feel the heat of her gaze on the side of his head and caught a whiff of her scent.

"I'm taking the little ones upstairs for a nap." She paused, as though she'd just looked at them and realized what was going on. "You boys don't need to be bothering Mr. Coblantz."

"They're not bothering me."

He wasn't going to, knew it was dumb, but he turned his head and looked at her, windblown, with rosy cheeks and a little one in each arm.

His cheek bunched and twitched, but he wouldn't allow himself to be swallowed up in longing for what might have been, could have been, if Cora had been different. Even though he'd found out this morning about Andrew's true father, he couldn't convince his stupid heart that he was better off without her.

She was feeling something, too, because her jaw jutted out. "Send them up if they start to be a pain."

An hour later, they were done with the second coat, and there wasn't anything more to do until it dried.

Well, there was plenty to do. No one had done any maintenance on the house in what looked like decades. Cora hadn't shown her face again, and while his mother had stirred herself to the restroom and the kitchen, she'd not been in a talkative mood, so Abner told the boys to put their coats on and took them to the hardware store with him.

He didn't mind. Kind of enjoyed having them. Before the accident that killed his dad and half-brother, he'd have figured by the time he was as old as he was, he'd have had six or seven kids of his own. Wanted them. Just something about a big house with activity and laughter. He'd always viewed it as a good thing. Couldn't wait until he had his own boys following him around the way he followed his dad. Had loved helping the eight little ones that had come after him.

Then the accident, leaving the Amish, and public school with the English. Then he'd fallen for Cora.

He'd never been able to look at anyone else.

"What are we getting?" Andrew asked, shoving his hands down in his pockets as a gust of wind kicked up. Looked like rain. Fitting for the viewing tonight, he supposed.

"Couple of doorknobs, and we're gonna see if they have the piece we need to fix the toilet to keep it from running all the time."

Andrew nodded thoughtfully, like he was considering the cost.

Both boys had told him they'd never been in the hardware store.

Brown leaves blew across the sidewalk along with an empty plastic bottle and someone's receipt as they turned the corner and headed down the main street in town. Clinton, OH, wasn't big enough for a stoplight, but it did have a hardware store, a post office, and a small diner. A gym. Several churches, one that looked like it was closed and one that had been turned into a craft store. A bar. A small convenience store with no gas pumps.

The boys walked beside him, looking around like they didn't usually walk down Main Street. Or maybe they hadn't lived here that long. He didn't know, and he wished he didn't care.

A horse with a wagon buggy was tied at the end of the street. It'd been years since he'd seen any of his Amish family, and of course, he didn't recognize the horse or the buggy. But chances were it'd be someone from his old community.

It was three buildings down from the hardware store, but it was also the only place he saw on either side of the street where a man could tie his horse, so whoever had the buggy could be anywhere.

Abner steeled himself. He'd killed his father and brother just as sure as if he'd put a bullet in them. The Amish weren't supposed to hold grudges, but they were human. He'd not been back to know how anyone felt.

The bell jingled overhead as he pulled the door open. The boys walked in and waited for him, sticking close to his side.

He nodded to the cashier, who, he suspected, was also the owner.

"Back for more?" the man said by way of greeting.

Abner jerked his head. He saw a straw hat sticking up over the shelves in the aisle he needed to go down. His gut wasn't giving him a good feeling about this, and he was tempted to leave. Maybe if he hadn't had Andrew and Derrick with him, he might have. But they were watching, and he needed to act like a man and not a coward.

He turned down the aisle that held the doorknobs. An Amishman with three small boys crowded around his legs stood looking at hinges. His face looked up, giving a neighborly nod, typical of small towns, before his gaze went back to the hinges. His face jerked back up, his eyes narrowed at Abner.

Despite the beard and glasses, Abner was almost sure it was one of his half-brothers. The man looked like a carbon copy of his father. And of Abner. Abner even had the beginnings of a beard to match him.

Eli, maybe.

"Ya look like my half-brother," the man said, his words heavy with the Pennsylvania Dutch accent typical of Amish but not colored with the twang that Abner had picked up.

Andrew and Derrick looked at him. He felt their gazes but focused on the man in front of him. "Abner," he said.

The man's gray eyes crinkled, then his teeth showed out of his hairy face. "It's Iddo. You remember me?"

The brother after Eli. "'Course I do. I taught you how to pound nails. You blackened both of my thumbnails, split the one clear in half. Man doesn't forget pain like that."

Iddo laughed, walking forward and holding out his hand, his kids crowding close behind. "Never met anyone with more patience than you." He clasped Abner's hand. "You never even looked annoyed. Had to've hurt."

"Did." Abner couldn't believe Iddo wasn't even a little standoffish. Like he didn't hold Abner responsible for two deaths in his family.

"Where ya been?"

"Out west, mostly."

"Back for the funeral?"

Abner nodded, not even surprised that Iddo knew his grandmother had died. There were things that had probably changed since Abner had left, but for not having phones or cars, there was a huge sense of community and everyone knew everything about everyone else. And the town.

"Sorry to hear about that." Iddo shook his head.

Abner wasn't going to beat around the bush. It was time to stop wondering. "I thought you'd be mad at me since it was my fault Dad and Abraham died."

Iddo's brows scrunched down. "You know we don't hold grudges."

"I know you're not supposed to."

Iddo grinned a little, admitting that Abner had insider knowledge. "I don't know anyone who is."

"Mamm?" Abner said, the first word he'd uttered as a small child coming easily to his tongue, though he hadn't spoken the PA Dutch of his childhood for more than a decade.

Iddo shrugged. "I'm sure somewhere it still hurts." Losing a child couldn't be easy. "But she married again and had her seventeenth baby just last spring." Iddo nodded. "She doesn't blame you."

"It was my fault."

"It was an accident."

Abner's lips tightened, but he didn't argue. It was an accident. One that he caused.

"I don't have any plans of visiting, but good to know," he finally said.

"You've got some half-brothers that would love to see ya." One of his boys moved against his leg, and he put a big, work-hardened hand on the boy's little hat. "We lost a dad and two brothers that day."

"Mamm told me she didn't want me."

"She was hurting. I think we all say things we don't really mean when we're in pain."

That was true. He'd done it himself. To Cora. But his Amish mother had not come and asked him to go back. Of course, what right did she have to ask him to leave the home of his "real" mother?

"You're right, but I don't see any point in going back."

"We're all scattered around, married, anyway."

"Good to hear you're doing well."

They talked for a bit more, but Abner didn't linger. It was getting late, and they needed to get ready for the viewing. Cora had a lot of work to do to get six small children fed and bathed and ready. He might not like her, but he could still help her.

Chapter 7

Cora woke with a start. Groggy. Not quite sure where she was. She hated that feeling.

Weights on her arms that were sticky with sweat reassured her that her children were snuggled next to her, sleeping. Summer and Kohlton. They were on Aunt Sandy's bed, with Claire in the crib beside them. Luna was curled in a ball at the bottom.

Cora's arms were numb, and her nose was itchy, but she didn't want to move and wake her kids. A mother with six children didn't wake them unless the house was on fire.

Her eyes flew open wide, and she yanked her head around, looking at the clock.

The viewing.

She'd overslept.

Rats. Rats. Rats.

She forced herself not to jump up. It was best to figure out first what she could do in the time she had left.

Baths. Everyone needed to be cleaned up.

Food. The kids would need to be fed.

Clothes. Had she figured out the underwear situation?

And the thought that made her sit up with a start: where were Derrick and Andrew?

Summer and Kohlton moaned and stretched as they slid off her arms. Cora scooted to the corner of the bed, careful to avoid Luna. She needed to make sure the boys were okay before she started dealing with the little ones.

Hurrying to the other bedroom, she peeked in. Empty.

Her heart pounded. Usually, the boys were in school, and she didn't have to worry about them. They'd been with Abner, but he hadn't said he would watch them. For all she knew, he could have left.

Pounding down the steps, she raced by the living room, noting that Aunt Sandy was at least sitting up, and into the kitchen.

She screeched to a halt.

Abner turned, spatula in hand. The table was set, and Andrew and Derrick were sitting at their places, eating.

"You slept forever, Mom," Andrew called from across the table.

"Yeah. We went up to check on you, and you didn't even wake up." Derrick held a spoonful of fried potatoes in front of him. "You were snoring."

Cora's cheeks heated. Why did she care that Abner might have heard her snore? She put a hand to her head. Her hair stuck out all over the place, straggling out of her messy bun. No worse than open-mouthed snores. She wiped her lips. Or the drool track on her cheek.

Yeah. It was a good thing she didn't like Abner and didn't care what he thought about her.

Although it was nice of him to cook supper and start feeding the boys. Watching them all afternoon.

"We went to the hardware store." Andrew's eyes gleamed.

"We fixed the toilet," Derrick added proudly.

"That's great. Thanks." She meant it, but her voice lacked enthusiasm, and she turned around without looking at Abner. She was a mess, and he made her feel like a failure.

She was a failure.

She'd managed to have six kids to three different men, and not one of those men could stand her long enough to stay more than a year. Meanwhile her kids hero-worshipped any man who paid the slightest bit of attention to them while she couldn't pull herself together long enough to have her family ready to attend the viewing of the woman who had been the closest thing they'd had to a grandmother.

Yeah. Definitely a failure.

Tears pricked at her eyes, and she fought them. She could cry later, but right now, she had a lot of work to do in the next forty-five minutes.

She needed the clean clothes that were in the bathroom slash laundry room off the other side of the kitchen.

Biting the insides of her cheeks and feeling like she was walking the gauntlet, she pivoted and strode to the door.

"Cora."

She wanted to ignore him. But her feet stopped without her telling them to.

Still, she wouldn't look at him.

"I'll help."

His words, only two, filled her chest and pushed her throat closed. She sucked in air.

"You've already cooked supper." She directed her words to the doorknob in front of her. Looked new. "That's more than enough."

Forcing her feet to move, she pushed through the door and grabbed the basket of clean clothes along with Abner's freshly washed laundry that she'd folded and put on the shelf. She set his things on the closed lid of the washer.

"Your clean clothes are in on the washer," she said.

"Thanks," he replied. "The boys took baths, but I didn't know what clothes you wanted them to wear. They said they didn't know, either."

"You two finish eating. I'll lay your clothes on your bed." She rushed out of the kitchen.

Aunt Sandy was just leaving the living room, and Cora almost collided with her. She shuffled the basket. "Sorry. Running late. But I ironed your dress last night and it's hanging behind my door."

Aunt Sandy nodded. "I'm getting a shower," she said in a voice that sounded rusty and sore.

Cora's heart sank. She should have showered while her kids were sleeping. She hadn't meant to fall asleep and be down all afternoon. Four of her kids needed to be bathed, too.

"Okay," she said in the most pleasant voice she could muster. "We'll be ready for the bathroom when you're done."

Aunt Sandy wasn't known for her quick showers or speedy beauty routine. Cora usually made sure she was done with the bathroom first. How had she managed to drop the ball today of all days?

Definitely Cora was not getting a shower before the viewing.

She hurried up the stairs; ten minutes had gone by, and all she accomplished was uniting her children with their clothes. But it was kind of dumb to put dirty kids in clean clothes.

"I'm hungry." Summer stood in the doorway of Aunt Sandy's room, rubbing her eyes.

Cora's stomach rumbled in response.

"You go on down to the table. Mr. Abner has cooked and your brothers are already eating." She was glad Abner hadn't waited on her to start feeding the kids.

Summer's lip stuck out, but she shuffled to the steps.

Kohlton's eyes were open, and his thumb was stuck in his mouth. "You want something to eat, sweetie?" she murmured as she stroked his hair. She was in a hurry, but from experience, she knew it was next to impossible to hurry sleepy children.

He nodded without moving the rest of his body. He was always slow to wake up.

"There's food downstairs." She scooped Luna up, who snuggled into her arms. With a glance at Claire, who was awake but not moving, she shifted Luna and picked up Kohlton.

Smiling and bouncing them, she carried them down the stairs, catching up to Summer and having them all laughing by the time they reached the kitchen.

When one of her boyfriends had left—she couldn't even remember which one—she had realized that the kids' moods depended almost solely on the adults' moods. It was one of the things she was trying to change about herself. She wasn't dependent on having a man to give her self-worth, and she could choose to be happy.

Funny how when she chose happiness, her kids did, too. They might be pressed for time, but they could still laugh. She shoved her irritation and anxiety out of the way and plopped Kohlton down in his seat.

Abner slid a plate in front of him before she even stood back up. He smelled like the wind and leaves and solid goodness. A different scent than she remembered from high school. Better. It felt like a scent she could depend on. She looked up at him and smiled. "Thank you," she said, sincerely, from her heart.

He returned her smile and her heart somersaulted while warmth spread through her chest. She'd never wanted to do this by herself. She'd always wanted to be part of a team. But she couldn't fool herself that Abner would want someone like her. Plus, there was the promise she'd made to herself to stand on her own.

Still, she couldn't deny his smile warmed her soul.

She put Luna in her booster seat and ran back up the stairs for Claire, whose fussing was getting louder and threatening to turn into full-on crying.

Her diaper was wet and needed to be changed, but Cora wanted to give her a bath, so she carried her downstairs, grabbing clothes and her baby towel. Feed her, bathe her, and then the baby would be done.

Still trying to figure out the logistics of how she'd get everyone else clean and fed, she nuzzled Claire's neck, blowing raspberries and getting Claire to decide to laugh rather than cry.

Out of breath, she hurried into the kitchen. All of her kids were eating. Whatever he'd made smelled good, and she remembered that she was hungry. She didn't have time to eat.

Strapping Claire into the highchair, she wondered if there were any vegetables in the fridge she could feed her.

Abner set a bowl down. "I mashed up some of the carrots and peas for her."

"Thank you." It was all she seemed to say to him. "I really appreciate your help."

"I've missed this."

"This craziness?"

"Since I left my Amish home, I've always wanted to be part of a big, busy family. Thanks for letting me."

Their eyes held for just a few moments. They could have been teenagers again with all the crazy things she was feeling in her chest.

She moved away, setting the towel and clothes on the counter and coming back to the other side of the highchair.

"I've got the kids, and I've already eaten. Grab something for yourself and eat." Abner's voice was full of command.

She didn't have time to eat. Walking to the sink, she grabbed the big dishpan that doubled as a baby bathtub out from the lower cupboard and turned the water on to rinse it out.

He'd washed the dishes, too.

She promised herself a good cry later. Maybe she and Abner wouldn't have worked out, but she'd been in love with him and thought he'd loved her, too. Things had changed when she'd done what she did because of Andrew, and it made her angry and sad and frustrated at the same time. Abner might have been her husband, and these could have all been their children, and this surreal experience of having another adult in the house who was actually helping her could have been her reality.

Could have been.

Dumb to even think it.

She dumped the water out of the tub and started filling it with warm water, tapping the stream with her wrist every once in a while to make sure it wasn't too hot or too cold.

When it was full, the kids were still eating. Abner sat by the high-chair feeding Claire. She didn't allow her eyes to linger on his big brown hands and the way they contrasted with her little pink baby. Wouldn't acknowledge the stirring in her chest and the longing that crept through her heart. The attraction that made her blood heat.

No. Not going there again. Not ever again.

"I'll be right back," she said and hustled out of the kitchen, taking the steps two at a time.

At least she didn't have to wonder what she was going to wear. She had one good skirt, black, thankfully, which was great for funerals and not so good for weddings, which suited her social schedule just fine since no one invited a single mother with six small children to their wedding anyway, and one nice top to wear with it. One pair of dress shoes. They were brown, but she wore them with her black skirt, defiantly, perhaps. Maybe someone would kidnap her and put her on one of those makeover shows on TV where they'd make fun of her fashion choices but provide a new wardrobe.

Wouldn't do her any good. She'd end up selling whatever clothes she came home with to buy things for her kids.

She could have finished her design project during naptime if she hadn't fallen asleep along with her kids.

Too late.

She threw her clothes on, ran a brush through her tangled hair, flipping it into a bun secured by elastic bands that wouldn't fall out if little hands grabbed it, and made a mental note to brush her teeth and wash her face downstairs while she was giving the kids a bath.

She laid all the clothes out for the kids, taking Luna's down with her so she wouldn't have to run back up the stairs for them.

Where had she left her purse? Her gaze swept the room, but she didn't see it. She'd have to check downstairs.

Rushing down, she hurried into the kitchen, passing Aunt Sandy headed up the stairs to change.

Abner stood at the sink, holding Claire in the dishpan as the baby splashed and cooed. He looked like he'd bathed a million babies as he swiped the washcloth under her chin, wiping along the deep wrinkles that were so easy to miss and down her tummy.

His hands weren't the hands of a man who worked in a daycare, and he'd said he didn't have children. Maybe he'd lived with a woman who had kids.

She didn't want to care, didn't want to like him, didn't want to feel anything for him, but she couldn't deny the curiosity that tumbled in her brain.

Couldn't get their few shared moments out of her head and didn't want to ignore the gratitude in her heart.

Remembering what he'd said about wanting the big family, she said, "You look like an expert at that." Then she hurried into the bathroom, scrubbing the kids down quickly and sending them up for their clothes. She almost had Andrew and Derrick help but realized that Abner had put them to work clearing off the table and doing the dishes in the sink beside the one he was bathing Claire in.

Fifteen minutes later, they were all ready. Abner was with them, and he, along with Aunt Sandy, stepped out with her and her children and walked slowly to the church where the only grandmother her children knew lay in a coffin.

Chapter 8

Officially, the viewing had been over for fifteen minutes. Unofficially, it was still going strong.

Abner stood in a corner, beyond the head of the body in the casket.

His grandmother had been a good woman, beloved in the church and respected in the community.

He'd watched as his birth mother greeted and spoke with the well-wishers. He didn't know most of them. This hadn't been the church he'd gone to nor had he lived in this town when he'd moved around with his mother after he left the Amish. She'd settled in with her mother sometime after he'd walked.

Doug, his other half-brother, had come in just a few minutes ago with his wife and two girls. Doug had recognized him but hadn't made his way over. Abner didn't go to him, content in his corner.

Watching.

Cora had rounded her children up and was getting ready to leave, carrying the two youngest.

He should help her.

But that unfamiliar anger swirled in his chest again.

Stephen had made an appearance.

He'd been as close to Stephen as he'd been to Doug and Jason. Which was to say not that close.

But the word had been that Cora had used Abner to catch Stephen's eye. She'd admitted it to him. When Abner had heard that she was pregnant, he'd always assumed the baby was Stephen's.

He was pretty sure Stephen was Derrick and Summer's father. Stephen had left the woman and cute little boys he'd arrived with to go over and pat those two on the head. He'd ignored Cora for the most part and walked back to his current family.

Abner had been annoyed at that but not angry.

The anger came when Cora's eyes had followed Stephen back to his wife and kids.

She'd managed to work beside Abner, getting her six kids ready for the funeral, and barely looked at him at all. But her eyes trailed after that man.

Abner blew out a breath, crossed his arms over his chest, keeping his gaze straight ahead, and wondered for the millionth time in two days why he couldn't get that woman out of his head and heart.

Doug had talked to Cora some. An animated conversation that seemed to drain the starch out of her shoulders and age her a decade. Abner would've liked to have heard what they said.

Doug finally made his way over, and they chatted. Not about Cora. Abner avoided mentioning her. Doug had helped set Cora up with Stephen while she was still seeing Abner, but Abner couldn't hold that against him all these years later. Having been raised by the Amish, Abner had been different. Too trusting, maybe. More interested in being a man than playing teenaged games. Maybe he'd been gullible.

It seemed ridiculous to hold a grudge. Especially since Doug had gone out of his way to call Abner and apologize.

So, they parted, if not friends, then at least no longer adversaries. Abner wasn't sure he'd ever see Doug again after the funeral tomorrow, and the reconciliation felt right.

When only the preacher and his mother were left, Abner left his post in the corner and walked to his mother's side. His brothers had left shortly after nine. Abner noted Jason had avoided Cora. She'd turned her back to him as soon as she saw him then proceeded to ignore him.

"Ready to go home, Mom?" he asked, putting his hand on her arm.

The pastor backed up respectfully. Abner had already spoken with him earlier.

Some of his Amish teaching had been easier to let go of than others. Humility before God and man had been one that he'd struggled with. The Amish didn't pray in front of people, and Abner had never even uttered the word "amen" with another person around.

Except in their own home, with their own family. It hadn't been a consideration for Abner, because he hadn't had a family of his own. Ever, really.

So, when the preacher asked him if he had anything to say at the funeral tomorrow, he'd declined. Nothing to say. Nothing to pray. He just wanted to leave.

His mother swallowed, her hands shaking. He'd guess she wanted a drink. He'd bet it wouldn't be too long from now and she'd be passed out on the couch. At least she was a quiet drunk.

She nodded, and he acknowledged the preacher with a tip of his head before he took her arm and walked out beside her.

The house was quiet, with only a light on in the kitchen when they walked in. Cora wasn't anywhere downstairs, so he assumed she'd gone to bed with her kids.

Or put them to bed and snuck out with someone.

No. He wouldn't think like that. Whatever she did was fine with him. And whatever she was, she was an excellent mother. He admired that about her. Wanted it in his own wife. Wished he'd had it growing up. She'd never leave her kids alone.

His mother set her purse on the table and collapsed into a chair. "I have a bottle upstairs in my closet. Go get it, son."

Abner stopped, his back to her, his hand on the faucet where he was just about to wash his hands.

He didn't want to judge. He'd seen the effects of alcohol and made a conscious and deliberate decision not to have it in his life. He'd felt it was the right one, despite the fact that it almost made drinkers angry to be around a non-drinker. He didn't care how angry people got. They were free to make their own decisions. As was he.

He didn't bash them for their decisions. But his mother? Especially since, from what he'd seen since he came, she was an alcoholic. Still, he couldn't deny her the crutch she needed since her mother was lying in state just a couple hundred yards away from where she sat and the casket would close forever on her body tomorrow.

He didn't want a drink, wasn't even tempted, but he did need a walk.

Without saying anything, he washed his hands, dried them, and walked out. Up the stairs.

Up to Cora.

It wasn't a mystery which room was his mother's. The door was open, and Cora sat on the bed, the blue light from her laptop filling the room.

"Knock, knock," he said softly.

Her eyes flew open, and her head yanked up. "What?" she whispered fiercely.

He stepped in. "Getting a bottle for my mom."

Her brows shot up, and he remembered the hard time he'd given her when she'd done the exact same thing. Maybe he'd come up here less on principle and more because he wanted to see Cora.

Disgusted with himself, he scanned the dark room, finding the door that must be the closet and getting the bottle from above the clothes rack easily.

He wanted to ask what she was doing, how she felt, what he could do tomorrow to help her, but she didn't want him, didn't even like him, and he didn't like her, either.

Just loved her as well.

She didn't say anything to him, but her eyes followed him.

He didn't owe her anything, but he said, "I'm going for a walk."

Her head jerked. "I have a design job I'm finishing."

He appreciated the consideration, since she didn't owe him.

He left without opening his mouth again, telling himself as soon as the funeral was over tomorrow, he was getting on his bike and pointing it west.

North Dakota called.

He kept his mouth shut when he set the bottle down in front of his mother on the table. Maybe he should try to comfort her, but they'd never been close. He couldn't remember her hugging him, even once. It would be weird to start tonight. The bottle seemed to be the only comfort she wanted anyway.

He couldn't leave, couldn't head west like he felt called to do, but he could at least get out.

The wind had picked up and the cold was biting, but he walked for several hours, hiking to the stone quarry he'd visited a time or two as a teen. Always in the summer.

There was a high wall and a deep pool below, black as tar on a night like tonight. Deep, dark blue on a sunny summer day. Deadly at any time. He knew of at least two kids who'd stepped off the cliff and into the clutch of eternity, hitting the water and never resurfacing.

He'd jumped a couple of times, but daredevil stunts were never a thrill to him. He did like the challenge, though. Working on a roof on a hot summer day, jumping off a cliff, or, apparently, mooning over a woman who saw every man but him as a potential bed partner and father.

He was so leaving tomorrow.

He didn't want her anyway.

Standing at the edge of the cliff, swaying slightly in the wind that howled down the ridge and tunneled along the high wall, he looked down into the darkness below. Knowing what was there, unable to actually see it, not needing to in order to know he was inches away from joining his grandmother, not tempted in the slightest to breech those inches, but not afraid, either.

He looked up at the night sky, at the high, gray clouds that raced across the moon, blocking even that light from illuminating the ground around. This wasn't North Dakota, but he felt closer to God out here than he had in the church. His fault, not God's. God was in the church, just the same as he was in the wind and the cliffs and the ridge and every space between. There was just less out here to distract him from noticing his Creator.

In the church, all he could see was Cora. All he could feel was his anger at what she'd done. All he could think was how much he loved her.

Here, he could feel God's spirit. See the truth. Hear the Word. It was all the same. Jesus was the Word. The Word was with God, and the Word was God. He didn't understand, but he knew it to be true just as sure as he knew one more step would plunge him into eternity.

The Bible was the Word. He believed that and read it daily. Only, he hadn't today.

The wind swirled. His jaw tightened. He swayed.

He hadn't read it, because he'd stopped at the beginning of Hosea.

A gust shook the bare branches on the ridge and whistled below his feet. Then, suddenly, there was silence. Complete quiet. Nothing moved, and he held his breath, waiting.

Long seconds passed. Abner couldn't even tell how much time slipped by with no sounds, no movement. Even the clouds seemed to stop.

He shook his head, turning on his boot. It caught on a loose stone as he pushed off. His foot slipped and he fell to his knee, the stone slipping off the edge and falling into the night. He never heard it hit.

His heart pounded and his knee burned as he rose slowly back to his feet. Not really fear but definitely adrenaline spiked his blood pressure.

Maybe God was trying to tell him something, maybe he was just homesick. He didn't know, and he started back.

It was well after midnight when he stood in front of his mother's house. One more night, then he was leaving.

But as he walked through the broken gate and up the path to the house, a squeaking sound came from behind the house.

Plenty of things could squeak in the night, and he shouldn't have thought a thing about it, but his feet took him off the path and around the house where Derrick and Andrew had run just yesterday when he'd first stood at the gate and just before he saw Cora for the first time in years.

She was on the kids' swing now, her hands gripping the chain and her cheek leaning against one of them, facing away from him. He watched her for a bit, wondering what she'd do if he walked over, placed his hands over hers, and bent down, kissing her temple and breathing in her scent. Standing behind her, giving her his heat.

He wanted to.

Despite everything he knew and everything he'd seen, he wanted to.

The girl he'd loved in high school was still there. Sweet and funny. Sassy. Cute and giving. It wouldn't be hard to fall for her again. She'd never left his heart anyway.

But he was leaving.

He turned, quietly and carefully, and walked back to the porch, noting the sagging gate, the rickety steps, and the porch that needed to be patched and painted.

He stepped in the hall and, from the light of the kitchen, saw the unfinished wall that had been spackled but not sponged off for the last time and still needed to be painted.

He couldn't leave a job unfinished.

And, yeah, maybe his mother hadn't been much of a mother to him, but it didn't excuse him for not being a good son. He could stay and fix a few things before he left.

Chapter 9

Cora woke to the smell of bacon and coffee. Funny how much easier it was to get up when her brain begged her body to follow her nose.

It also felt good that she'd gotten her project done the night before and sent it off to be approved.

Of course, what Doug had told her at the viewing had spoiled most of her plans, and she didn't know what to do.

She'd sent a couple of text messages off to friends, including one to Bob Price. She didn't really want to take him up on his offer, but since Doug had said he truly was taking Aunt Sandy back to North Carolina with him, she needed to find another place to live. Fast.

She already knew she couldn't afford a house. A two-bedroom apartment might work. If she could find one cheap enough, she could put the kids in the bedrooms and sleep on the couch. She'd spent a lot of time trying to figure something out last night after she'd finished her project. Abner had been gone, and she'd spent some time wondering about that, too. Said he was taking a walk. There weren't exactly a lot of places one could hang out in town. Maybe he'd gone somewhere with someone else.

It was almost two a.m. when she'd gone in, and he'd been in the recliner in the living room. It was hard to tell herself she didn't care, because she knew she did.

Thinking about Abner wasn't going to help her find a house.

She could think about it later. After coffee.

Aunt Sandy was actually up when Cora went down, with Luna on one hip and Claire on another. She was sitting at the table, a cup of coffee in her hand.

Her eyes were bloodshot and ringed with dark circles. Her hands shook as they lifted the coffee cup to her mouth, and she'd slept in the clothes she'd worn to the viewing.

But she was up. Unusual for sure.

Abner stood at the stove with his back to her.

"Good morning, Aunt Sandy," Cora said, setting Luna in her booster seat before strapping Claire into her highchair.

"Morning, Cora." Abner's voice came over her shoulder. She didn't want the shiver that curled her toes and made her fingers tingle.

Ugh. She wanted to bite her tongue. He said a simple good morning; why couldn't she respond in kind?

Because she wanted to know where he was last night. Or maybe there was something wrong with her. Maybe she'd never forgiven him for leaving without giving her a chance to tell him what had actually happened.

She was partly to blame, but he'd left.

Her mouth opened and she forced the words out. "Good morning, Abner. Out ramming around until pretty late last night." That was more than she wanted to say.

"I *was* out 'ramming' around. I almost left."

What did he mean by that? She snapped the buckle on the booster seat. Abner set a plate with eggs, toast, and bacon down in front of her seat.

"I'm sorry. Thank you so much for everything that you've done since you've come." She managed to get the words out of her mouth, but she couldn't look at him as she said them. "It's none of my business what you were doing. I don't know why I said that."

"It's because he left you." Aunt Sandy's coffee cup clanked down on the table. Her bloodshot eyes looked Cora up and down. "Things would have been a lot different if he'd'a stayed." Her head shook. "Men. Pride makes them stupid."

Cora could agree with that to some extent. Abner had a lot of pride.

But he wasn't the only one in the room who had been stupid. She'd been a lot dumber for a lot longer, and she couldn't let his mother sit there and insult only him.

"It's not all his fault, Aunt Sandy. He didn't know everything, and I had too much pride to tell it all to him." That wasn't entirely true. She'd had every intention of telling him every sordid detail. But hadn't gotten her nerve up before he left. She'd been worried he'd be disgusted. Hate her.

Then he'd been gone, and it hadn't mattered.

"What didn't you tell me?" Abner asked softly. His voice was almost gentle, but when she looked up at him, the hardness in his eyes was still there.

He didn't believe her. Didn't believe that there was anything she hadn't said. Or maybe he thought what she hadn't said was worse than what she had.

It was. But not in the way he thought.

Derrick and Andrew came into the kitchen, saving her from answering. Summer and Kohlton came not long afterwards, and things were crazy from then on until it was time to leave the house for the funeral at eleven.

Chapter 10

Abner walked out of the house with Claire in one arm and Kohlton holding tight to his other one. She held Summer's hand and carried Luna. The boys walked on either side of Aunt Sandy, who was as sober as Cora had ever seen her.

She could almost pretend they were a family. After their tense exchange at the breakfast table, they'd been able to work together to get the kids ready again.

If she didn't harbor so many complicated feelings about Abner, she'd think he was nice.

Their timing stank, though, since Jason and his family pulled into the church lot as they were walking in.

"Don't squeeze so hard, Mommy," Summer said.

"Sorry, sweetie," Cora murmured.

Really? Of all the times in the world they could show up, it had to be at the same time she and her children did.

She tried to hurry her children along, so they'd get in the church first, but a two-year-old could only walk so fast.

If Abner noticed her distress, he didn't say anything, which was probably best, since they could hardly fight if they weren't talking to each other.

Jason and his wife were out of their car and hit the church steps right behind Cora and her kids. She didn't turn around to greet him, although Aunt Sandy stopped to say hi to her son.

She walked into the church, breathing in the scent of hymnbooks and Bibles and the faint smell of coffee. Furniture polish. There was only one full pew left that had been saved for family, and Cora began arranging her children in it.

But Abner wasn't behind her like she'd assumed. She sat Luna and Claire on the seat, putting Derrick and Andrew on the end and leaving enough room for two more little bodies. She looked around.

Abner was in the back, talking to Jason's wife, Erin.

Well, hopefully he would drop her kids off when he was finished. She turned and sat.

Jason slid in beside her. Her entire body froze.

"Hey, Cora."

No. She wasn't doing it. Years ago, she'd kept her mouth shut to protect her half-sister. Her silence didn't mean that what he'd done was okay. She wasn't sitting beside him.

Conscious that they were in the front and it would look bad if she popped up like toast out of a toaster, she counted slowly to ten before she moved to stand.

He put his fingers on her arm. "Ignoring me?" he said softly. "Why? We used to have fun together."

She continued to straighten, and his fingers tightened before they fell off.

The pianist played softly. Sweet hymns that floated gently through the sanctuary of mourners. Cora was no longer noticing that, nor the murmurs and movement of others around her.

Her sole focus was getting away.

"Excuse me." The voice, coming from behind her, was familiar and welcome.

She turned in time to see Abner moving past Jason and sliding in behind her. She felt his heat at the same time she caught his scent, masculine and rugged, though somehow not at odds with their environment. A complement to it.

She didn't take the time to try to figure out the apparent contradiction, and she didn't try to hide her relief, either.

Luna's arms reached up for Abner, and he picked her up, brushing against Cora and making her uncomfortable in a deliciously distracting way, one that she really didn't want to acknowledge.

Much better than the creepy vibe she'd been getting from Jason. Memories she'd rather not relive.

"I'll sit here." His eyes searched hers like he might be realizing that everything he thought he knew wasn't all there was to know, but it was probably wishful thinking on her part. Too late now to change anything anyway.

"Thanks," she said simply.

His eyes narrowed, and he pitched his voice low, for her ears only. "I think it might be time for us to talk. Later."

Pulling her lip back, she shook her head. Too late. Too late. Too late.

The funeral was blessedly short, and there was no graveside service, but there was a meal afterwards. Aunt Sandy sat with Jason and Doug while Abner helped Cora, almost like they were married and her six children were theirs.

Everything was so much easier with a man beside her. But she couldn't let herself get used to it. She'd quit this game.

Maybe not if a man like Abner were interested.

Except she'd promised herself.

Of course, she'd do whatever was necessary to put a roof over her children's heads.

Thinking of that, she looked around for Bob. He wasn't hard to look at, and he'd offered her a place to stay. He hadn't responded to her text or email, but he wasn't much for writing, so it wouldn't surprise her if he just showed up. He was a firefighter and worked odd hours, so maybe he was on call and couldn't.

Her stomach curled, and she tried to calm herself. Something would work out. She'd make it.

Since her project was finished and she hadn't gotten another one, she'd search the internet tonight after the kids went to bed to see if she could find a place. She hated to move them out of the school district, but if she had to, she would.

By the time the meal was over, her children were fussy and needed naps.

Abner, holding Luna, had stopped to talk to an older lady with a cane. Cora didn't recognize her, and Claire needed a diaper change, so she kept going, holding tight to Kohlton's hand, Summer trailing behind.

Jason and Doug met her at the door.

"We need to talk to you," Doug said, serious but not unkind.

Jason had more of a smirk. "About your living arrangements."

"I understand Aunt Sandy is moving out." She hadn't wanted to be confronted about it again, after what Doug had said last night, but figured she needed to face this head-on.

"Rent's paid until the end of the month. You need to be out by then."

"I figured."

"I'll be taking Aunt Sandy down with me when I leave tomorrow." Doug put his hands in his pockets and rocked back on his feet. "My wife's tired, and she wanted to rest in our hotel this evening, so I thought you could help her pack."

Cora bit the insides of her cheeks. She was tired, too. And Aunt Sandy was their mother. But Aunt Sandy had done so much for her. She was also Abner's mother and Abner had been nothing but helpful to Cora. Cora could do this one thing. Not for Doug and Jason. But for Abner and Aunt Sandy. "Of course. I'll work at it this afternoon and have things ready to go tonight."

"That'd be great. I might stop in then, this evening, that way we can leave straight from the hotel tomorrow." Some of the tension in Doug's shoulders eased, like he'd been afraid Cora would give him a hard time.

"I'll make sure everything is ready." Claire wiggled in her arms, and Cora juggled her while keeping a hold on Kohlton's hand. He pulled against it and swung back and forth, but she'd been doing this for years and barely noticed. As long as he wasn't running around knocking people down, he could do a little swinging on her arm.

Jason clapped Doug on the shoulder. "Hey, Doug, you go on and see about getting Mom. I want to talk to Cora for a minute."

"Sure, Jason. I'll meet you in a bit. I have numbers for two treatment centers." Doug walked away.

Cora lifted her brows. "So, she's getting some help?"

"It's pretty obvious she needs it." Jason's gaze didn't meet hers but settled somewhere lower. She tried not to squirm, feeling that's what he wanted.

She started to move away.

He shifted. "I have a place where you can stay."

This wasn't something she wanted to listen to. If it were her, she'd sleep on the street first. But she had her children to consider.

"We used to have a good time together." Maybe he thought his voice sounded sexy. To her much younger self, it had. Not anymore.

"*You* used to have a good time."

His face jerked back like he was surprised. "Everything we did was consensual."

"It was." She forced the words out because they were the truth.

"And you were above the age of consent."

"I was." That was true too.

"Then why are you acting like I've done something wrong?"

"You cheated on your wife."

"And you were the other woman."

Like she needed to be reminded.

"Erin never found out, and it didn't hurt anyone." His voice dropped. "You look like you could use a good time."

If he thought for one second that what they'd done hadn't been wrong, there was no point in her arguing. Just like there was no point in her trying to explain to him that she'd been young and stupid and infatuated and had stars in her eyes about the older, handsome man that'd been interested in her.

She'd been dumb as dirt. Hopefully she'd gotten smarter. If she had she needed to show it.

"I have six kids. I can't even believe you're hitting on me."

"You don't look like you've had six kids. You look good." His hand settled on her arm.

She wasn't under any illusions that she was anything special to him. He was a ladies' man and a player, and she was one of the few women under sixty at the service.

She didn't want to make a scene in getting away from him, but his hand tightened on her arm.

Heat at her back made her want to turn, but then Abner's voice came from above her shoulder and she didn't have to.

"I'm thinking the lady wants to leave."

She didn't turn to see what expression Abner had on his face as he looked at his half-brother, but it must have been something intense, because Jason's jaw hung open and his hand dropped from her arm.

She'd have to remember to thank Abner later. So much to thank him for.

"I need to put my children to bed." This time, she pushed through, and he stepped back, giving her space. Man, she hoped she could come up with a place to live.

Chapter 11

Abner had stayed after the dinner with Andrew and Derrick and helped the church ladies clean up and move the tables and chairs back. For the most part, Luna had been content to ride on his shoulders.

He couldn't help walking over when he'd seen Cora talking to Jason again. She seemed to be handling herself okay, and he'd already pushed in more than she probably wanted when he sat beside her before the service. But she seemed relieved and grateful and he was glad he had.

Maybe he should be thinking more about his mother and his grandmother, but neither one had been a big influence in his life, and he wasn't going to fake feelings he didn't feel. He'd do his duty. Appreciate the small part they played. But any intense sadness, or, God forbid, tears, would be contrived.

It was warm for November, probably in the sixties, if he had to guess, and he enjoyed the deep blue sky and calm breeze as he walked back from the church with Luna still on his shoulders and Andrew and Derrick kicking stones along the road.

Doug had told him that his mom was leaving tonight. He supposed he should consider doing the same. Except, as much as the open sky and flat prairie of North Dakota was calling him, he didn't want to leave...Cora.

But he'd done it once before. He could do it again.

Except he really did want to talk to her. He kept getting the feeling he'd been wrong all those years ago. About something. He'd missed something. He needed to find out what it was.

"We're gonna play on the swing set," Andrew yelled and ran around the side of the house.

It reminded Abner of Cora sitting on the swing late last night. He wished now he'd gone to her and actually tried to have an adult conversation.

Not liking her was safer. Blaming her took his attention off his own faults. Wanting her was a given, but something he felt he needed to fight.

He lifted Luna off his shoulders and dropped her into the crook of his arm where she snuggled, sleepy. He admired the heart-shaped face that was all Cora's before he opened the front door and stepped in.

His mother sat on the steps, still wearing the outfit she'd worn at the funeral, a can of beer in her hand.

Cora, in worn jeans with holes in both knees and a loose long-sleeved tee, her hair in a long braid hanging over her shoulder, was coming down the stairs with a suitcase in one hand and a large black trash bag in the other. It bulged, looking heavy.

"I'd get that for you." Irritation laced his voice. Why was she trying to do this all herself? She knew by now he'd help.

"I know." She barely looked up, concentrating on slipping around his mother, who didn't seem like she was even considering moving. "But I can get it myself."

Luna was too big to be held like a baby, but he tucked her tight against him and reached his hand out, sliding it onto the suitcase handle beside hers. "Let go. I've got it."

He didn't look at her, staring instead at the differences in their fingers. Hers tapered and white, his rough and brown.

"I said I could do it myself." She hadn't raised her voice, but there was an edge that hadn't been there before.

He should let it go, he knew he should, but that stubborn determination that he'd never quite beat into submission reared its head.

"And I said, let go."

"You know, son. Cora's a nice girl. But she's got six kids, and that's not going to be a walk in the park for any man. You oughta find someone a little easier." His mother didn't turn her head, nor did she slide out of the way so Cora could get through.

She took a long drink of her beer, wiping her mouth with the back of her hand and dropping her arm back into her lap.

Cora's body seemed to shrink, and she pulled both lips between her teeth. But her back straightened, and her eyes narrowed.

She didn't look at him, but he stared straight into her eyes, remembering the cliff edge of the night before and the feeling of standing next to the abyss. "Guess it's a good thing I'm not looking for a walk in the park."

Cora swallowed, loud in the silence that followed his words. Her eyes remained cast down, but her fingers slid off the suitcase handle.

Abner lifted it up and over his mother's head, setting it down at the foot of the stairs. Luna shifted in his arms, and Cora's eyes went to her daughter. Maybe her face softened a little.

"Hand me the bag," he commanded. Maybe he didn't have the right to tell her what to do, but he'd never be the kind of guy who sat around and waited for someone else to take charge.

Cora gave his mother a dubious glance before taking both hands and lifting the bag.

"Duck," he said to his mother.

To his surprise, she actually listened, and he was able to grab the bag, which seemed to be full of clothes, and sail it over her head.

"You have more stuff to bring down?"

Cora nodded. "A few boxes and another suitcase."

"Here." He nodded at Luna, snuggled against him, and lifted his arm a little. "You take her. I'll carry everything."

She hesitated, biting her lip.

"Come on. Let me get it." His tone was more commanding than he intended. But, seriously, did she expect him to watch while she lugged the stuff downstairs?

"Maybe I like the way you look holding her." Cora tilted her head and lifted a brow as though daring him to call her out on what had to be the first somewhat flirty thing she'd said to him since he came.

He ground his teeth together so his jaw didn't drop to the ground as his stomach whirled like a tornado and heat spread through his chest.

He could no more stop his next words than he could stop breathing. "I don't look near as good as you do."

Cora's eyes widened, and he realized he'd helped with her kids a lot, but he'd not complimented her at all. Her reaction made him think that she'd appreciate a few kind words from him.

"You'll look better if you flex your muscles while you're carrying my stuff down." His mother took another swig of her beer. "You two are so cute. Don't even like each other most of the day. Then whew." She fanned herself. "Hot as heck."

One side of Abner's lip curled up. She was right, as much as he didn't want to admit it. He met Cora's gaze. Her cheeks were red.

"Hot?" He didn't allow his half-grin to become a smirk as he lifted a brow at Cora.

Her eyes danced as she replied, "As heck."

He grunted. That was the Cora he remembered. Funny and cute. Sassy.

She held her arms out, and he carefully set Luna in them. Luna scrunched her face up like she maybe didn't want to leave him, but then she snuggled down in her mother's arms.

"You're an amazing mother," he murmured.

When Cora looked up, he realized he'd been standing there looking at her for enough seconds to make it obvious he was staring. He swallowed against the tightness in his throat and took a deep breath through his nose. He wanted to hold onto the moment when there was something shimmering between them that wasn't animosity and felt like it could be the start of something rekindled.

But the lucid part of his brain was telling him that was a really bad idea.

Maybe Cora saw the shift in him, or maybe she realized the same thing he did, but her eyes dropped.

"You'd make a really good father," she said.

Hardly flirting words. But maybe, at their age and position in life, a compliment on parenthood meant a lot more than a compliment on something as transient as looks or clothes.

She cradled her babe and moved away. His hand itched to bring her back.

He fisted it and turned, taking the stairs two at a time.

By the time he made it back down the stairs, he was all business. "Mom, what about the pots and pans in the kitchen, the furniture, the—"

His mom waved her hand. "The truck's coming after Thanksgiving. They'll get it. I'm leaving the dishes. Don't need 'em. Taking the TV and the couch, my bed."

"Okay." Abner wanted to look at Cora, but he couldn't bring himself to do so. She was losing almost everything.

He'd just had the worst feeling that maybe she'd been nice to him because she wanted to use him. Again.

AUNT SANDY LEFT WITH little fanfare.

Abner hadn't seemed to care. Cora supposed he felt about the same toward his mother as she did toward hers. She'd never earned the right to be her mom.

Cora wanted to be something different, better, for her own children.

After she had the kids in bed, she looked for places for rent in the area. The project she'd turned in had been approved, and the money had hit her account, but even if she could get another project done before the end of the month, it wasn't going to give her enough money to do first and last month's rent plus a security deposit on anything bigger than a two-bedroom apartment in Huntingdon, fifty miles away.

Her kids would have to change schools. It would be in the seedy part of town. She wouldn't know anyone.

Depressed, she bid on three more projects, thinking it'd be really funny if she got them all and couldn't do them but desperate to cast a wide net and at least get work, closed her laptop, and slipped out of bed.

Her clock said one a.m.

Abner was surely sleeping. She didn't know, since she'd walked up with her kids after supper and never walked back down. He'd said he wanted to talk to her. Honestly, she wished he'd just go. He didn't like her, and her attraction to him was exciting, but also annoying. Seeing how good he was with her children and having him help her just made her long for things she was never going to have because of the choices she'd made.

She didn't have time to deal with a man, and she'd sworn off boyfriends anyway.

Children first.

Grabbing a beanie hat and a hooded sweatshirt and still wearing her jeans and long tee from earlier, she slipped out the front door, not wanting to risk waking Abner up but needing to get some air.

She had no idea what she was going to do, and it was impossible to ignore the ball of fire in her stomach that felt very much like consuming fear.

Slipping around back, she sat in the kids' swing. There was something about that rocking motion that always seemed to soothe her, and feeling the cool night air, with the darkness hiding most of the daytime distractions, she felt closer to the Lord.

But her heart was too heavy to form words, and how could she ask for His help, anyway? It was her own choices that had gotten her to the mess she was in.

She'd swung back and forth about three times when a shadow by the pole moved.

She gasped.

"Didn't think you were coming out." Abner's voice was deep and low.

Her heart stumbled. "You've been waiting?"

"Said I wanted to talk."

Her hands tightened on the swing chain. She'd wanted to come out and let her guard down for a bit, but instead she needed to marshal her defenses.

"What?" he asked.

She hadn't said anything and didn't know what he was asking.

"Why did it look like you turned into a rag doll there for a minute?" He paused. "Hate the idea of talking to me that much?"

She didn't want to lie. She'd told a big one once, but among her sins, lying wasn't something she usually struggled with. "It's not on my Christmas wish list."

"Oh?" The moon came out from behind low, flat clouds. He crossed his arms over his chest. "What is on your wish list?"

Snapping out that it wasn't any of his business was what she wanted to do, to protect herself from the sweet longing he stirred in her, but she was too worn out to fight. She didn't want to anyway. Not with Abner.

"Obviously I need a place to live. But Christmas is too late. That's the Thanksgiving list."

"Neat. We get to make lists for Thanksgiving now, too?"

Something told her it'd been just as long since he'd gotten a Christmas gift as it had been for her. He hadn't had the stress of doing Christmas with small children.

Different choices.

She had to own hers.

"Sure. Why not?" Thanksgiving lists would be just as effective for her as Christmas lists.

"What else?" He hadn't moved, and she wished he'd look somewhere other than her. The moonlight didn't allow her to hide.

"I'd like steady work."

"Who would watch your kids?"

"I do graphic design online."

"That's what you were doing tonight?"

"No. I bid on a few jobs and looked for a place to live."

"Find anything?"

"Not yet. Not around here." She didn't want him to feel bad for her and decide he needed to fix it somehow. "I have someone who's offered me a place to stay. I just haven't been able to get a hold of him yet."

He stiffened, and the relaxed air was gone. "Him?"

"A friend."

"The father of any of your kids?"

"No."

"A new dad."

She stood abruptly. It felt like he was judging her. And although she deserved it to some extent, she'd made changes and was trying to stick to them.

"Good night." She twisted and started walking away.

"I'm sorry," he said immediately.

Her feet stopped. She wanted to keep walking. Needed to. This was always her problem. A sweet-talking man came along, and she gave in and did whatever he wanted. She couldn't do that anymore. Wouldn't do it. Maybe Abner was different. Her heart said he was. But she couldn't trust her heart. It'd been wrong so many times.

She didn't move.

COWBOYS DON'T MARRY THEIR ENEMY   87

"That wasn't what I wanted to talk about. And, you're right. You don't have to stay here and take it. It was rude of me."

"I'm sorry. I'm sensitive. I'm trying to change and I want to look forward, not back." She didn't turn around, but she was even less inclined to go. She wanted to believe him.

"I got the feeling there were things I didn't know or didn't understand from years ago. I was hoping you would help me."

"It's too late now, and it doesn't matter."

"It does to me."

"What do you want to know?" She wanted him to know everything. But she didn't trust him enough, didn't feel secure enough, knew he already didn't like her...there wasn't enough of a bond between them for her to spill her deepest secrets. She didn't know what he would do with them. The possibility that he would judge her and leave was sharply clear.

"Andrew is the child you told everyone was mine."

"Yes."

"Jason is his father."

"Yes."

He shifted, like he was uncomfortable. There was no way he could be more uncomfortable than her.

The fence wasn't much, especially around the side of the lot, but it was at least something to grab a hold of. She turned and walked through the spongy grass, putting a hand on a rickety picket.

She hadn't heard him follow her, but suddenly, he was there, in front of her, his hand on the picket next to hers and his eyes searching down into her soul.

"We were together, and you were with Jason?" The question was ragged. The pain was real, and it surprised her. So much time had passed, and it still hurt. She'd been the one falling for Abner. She hadn't believed he'd cared that much about her.

"It wasn't like that."

"You were pregnant with his kid." The picket snapped under his fingers. "How could it not be like that?"

She set her jaw and crossed her arms. "You're not listening. You've already judged me."

He let out a harsh breath, running a hand through his hair and turning away from her. "Tell me what it was then, Cora. Make me see."

Her throat closed, and she fought back the urge to cry. She didn't have an excuse. She'd been young and stupid, but putting those words out on the air, exposing them to his ridicule and judgment, felt too raw and too hard.

He turned and took both her upper arms in his hands, not gripping hard but a firm grasp. "I'd fallen for you. I'd have done anything for you. But you were sleeping with another man and using me to get to my cousin, then you lied about me on top of it all. How much can a man take?"

He held her arms with all the suppressed energy of tectonic plates with a fraction of an inch left to shift before an earthquake exploded out of the ground.

He looked at the sky, like he wished he hadn't said anything, dropped his hands, and turned.

The breeze shifted the bare branches, and something rattled at the back of the house. A loose piece of siding, maybe. Nothing she'd have to worry about in two weeks.

"You wouldn't have done anything for me," she said softly, grateful he'd turned, because she'd been unable to stop the overflowing of her right eye. The tear tracked down her cheek, but her voice remained steady.

"Yes, I would have."

"I told everyone the baby was yours. I didn't realize it would get back to you before I got a chance to explain to you what happened." Her voice was whisper soft, barely audible above the swish of the leaves on the ground. "I hoped you'd marry me."

"Make me understand how you think that would have happened."

"Maybe that's why I waited too long. Because I was scared you'd be like you are right now. Angry."

"It might look like anger to you, but it feels like pain to me."

Cora brushed the tear off her cheek and willed herself not to let any more fall. She'd cried enough to last a lifetime.

"I thought you loved me," she said, her voice thin.

"Love's blind, not stupid."

Ouch. That hurt. As he intended, she was sure. She couldn't doubt he was hurting, had been hurting all these years. As she had.

"I thought if you loved me, you'd come to me and find out the truth. Instead, you left."

He spun around. "Feels like we're talking in circles, because we're back to the fact that you were pregnant with another man's child. Maybe it makes me weird, but that told me loud and clear that you weren't interested in me. Only using me to protect him." His jaw hardened. "Unless he raped you. If he did—"

"He didn't." She had to be clear about that. It might be tempting to lay all the blame at Jason's feet, but that would be the coward's way out. She'd known what she was doing. She'd just been stupid. Stupidity wasn't an excuse to blame someone else.

Her feet had taken a step back. Abner hadn't raised his voice at all, but the tension coming off him felt sharp, like daggers in the night.

"I'm sorry. At the time, I thought you'd understand. I can see now, there was nothing for you to see."

She stopped.

"Keep talking."

"I was living in his house." She shrugged. "He was handsome and charming, an older man showering attention on me. I believed him when he said his marriage was over, he was leaving her, they weren't happy, all those things men say and they don't mean. Lies. I believed them." Her voice held bitterness, and she stopped to try to wrestle it back under control.

He shoved his hands in his pockets and didn't say anything.

It was a good minute of silence between them before she went on. "I'd figured out that Jason was lying, but I didn't have anywhere to go, and I was afraid to tell him no. I needed out. I didn't know I was pregnant."

She crossed her arms over her chest and shoved her hands in her armpits, hunkering down inside her coat as the breeze blew again. Her stomach curled and cramped.

Abner could have been a statue. His hair wasn't even long enough to move in the wind.

If he was impatient to know the rest of the story, she couldn't tell.

"Stephen and I had talked some, and I knew he was interested in me. He had his own place, and I could have moved out of Jason and Erin's house. But I didn't have a way to get to him, and I couldn't just go up and tell him I wanted to move in with him. So, yeah. I used you. I knew if I was with you, I'd see Stephen."

Abner made a sound, a groan, maybe, on an expelled breath.

She wished he'd say something, but she supposed she ought to finish her story, even if it had gotten harder with his silence.

She fisted her hands under her armpits.

"I wasn't planning on falling for you. But I had. We'd known each other for a long time. You shared some of the same issues with your parents, your mother especially, that I did, and when we were finally together...well, it was easy to fall in love with you."

She kicked at the grass, dropping her eyes. "When Erin found the pregnancy test box in the bathroom trash can, I had to name a father." Lying wasn't something she did, not before that night and not after. "I couldn't look her in the eye and tell her I was pregnant with her husband's child. I might have been young and dumb, but I knew it was wrong, and I didn't want to hurt her." Lying was wrong. Every day, all day long. But she couldn't regret that one. "I'd been aiming for Stephen. After you left, we did get together, but that night, standing in front of her, your name is the one that came out of my mouth. Because you're the one I wanted."

Abner's hands were still in his pockets. He stood facing the house. His head dropped down, like he could see the ground and was counting blades of grass.

After long moments of silence, he finally said, "Thanks for telling me."

That was it? That was all he was going to say? She'd just told him everything in her heart, and he couldn't think of anything to say in reply?

Heat swept over the back of her neck and up her temples. Her eyes narrowed.

Abner moved. His hands stayed in his pockets, but he shifted so his body faced hers. "I know that wasn't easy for you. I'm pretty angry at myself right now, because you were right. I can see how things might have turned out a lot different if I hadn't been so sure I was right and left without talking to you."

She turned her head to the side and scuffed the grass with her foot. "I should have made a harder effort to see you and not been a coward."

"I guess we both deserve to take some of the blame. But the bulk of it falls on me. I never dreamed, in all the time between then and just now, that would be true." He pulled a hand out of his pocket and touched her shoulder. "I'm sorry."

She couldn't doubt his sincerity.

It made it easier for her to explain everything else. "I...I guess after that, I let myself get caught up in needing to have a man beside me. Maybe it was proof that someone loved me. Maybe it was a security thing because after I hit my teens, I was never sure what house I'd be staying in. Maybe I just have some kind of personality flaw, but I couldn't be alone, and I made a lot of bad choices because of that."

She was talking about the children she had and the men she'd been with. Somehow it seemed important that Abner know.

"Maybe that wouldn't have happened if I'd made one different choice."

She wouldn't allow him to shoulder all the blame. "I guess that's possible. But every choice I made is mine. I have to own them. After the last guy left, it was clear. I needed to be sober, and I needed to stop depending on men to help me or make me feel worthy or good or whatever. My kids come first. No more alcohol. No more men."

That's exactly what she'd decided. She thought it was a good decision, and she thought Abner would agree.

But there was no flash of teeth in the moonlight. No turned-up lips. His gaze seemed sad and serious as he stared down at her. Maybe he was still thinking about what might have been. He shouldn't.

"I regret the sin. It always bites. But I don't regret my children. I just feel bad that I haven't been a better, more responsible parent. I decided to change, and so far, it's worked." She deliberately lightened her voice. "I guess it's none of my business, but I just bared my whole sordid history to you. Tell me about you. You're so good with kids. You must have lived with someone who had them or had a girlfriend with a few."

"No."

Her eyes swept over his face, and her smile faded. He didn't seem inclined to elaborate, and her lips pressed together. Surely it wouldn't be that hard for him to give her a little of his history, make her feel less exposed.

But he didn't say anything, so she asked, "Where'd you get so good with kids?"

"Until I was thirteen, I had little brothers and sisters."

She hated the way he said that. Like somehow one had brothers and sisters, then one didn't.

Her heart broke for him, just a bit. Wished she could have made different choices. She wanted to be the one to fill his need for a partner.

To walk this life beside him. But she was too messed up to be of any good to anyone, let alone a man like Abner.

How different her life might have been if she'd been raised in a home with a mom and a dad who cared for her, rather than living in her half-sister's basement and becoming enamored with her husband.

Chapter 12

Cora didn't want a man.

He couldn't blame her for swearing off men. He'd be afraid if he were her too. Afraid of choosing another man who was just going to leave. Seemed like she'd had a pile of guys, but no good ones.

His heart still hadn't settled down, pounding in an angry rhythm, and his neck was hot. Anger at himself. He couldn't unclench his jaw.

Why hadn't he gone and gotten the story from her?

He could ask that question all day long, but he knew. He *knew*.

Pride.

He'd been hurt, hearing that she was pregnant. The idea of her with another man. It had burned like peeling membranes off his heart. Like wire in his veins. Like a stiff-bristled brush over third-degree burns.

He could take the pain. He would have.

But he couldn't stand the thought that she'd cheated on him. That she'd used him, toyed with him, that he'd walked with her, his heart in his eyes and on his sleeve, told her things no one else knew, and she hadn't cared, wanted someone else instead.

His pride had been wounded, and he thought he'd walked away with dignity, but he'd slunk away like a coward, because he didn't want to go to her and have her laugh in his face. Hadn't wanted to risk the rejection.

A real fear.

One he should have faced.

But he'd run instead.

He'd already apologized.

Everything that had happened to her since then had hinged on that one decision of his—the decision to believe the worst and walk away.

94

And now, he was back, having never stopped wanting her. But she didn't want a man.

Maybe he could change her mind.

"I'd like a chance to be your friend." It was the only thing he could think of to say.

Her head snapped up. Her eyes were wide. But the moonlight shone on her cheekbones, emphasizing the heart shape of her face, and he remembered another night, what seemed like a lifetime ago, when they'd strolled under the stars together, along the railroad tracks in the moonlight. They'd walked on the rails, keeping their balance and seeing how fast they could go. Something so simple, but they'd laughed and had fun, and he'd loved her easy laughter and how she didn't need anything fancy to be happy.

"I've sworn off men."

"I'm not asking to be your man. I'm asking to be your friend."

"I think friendship is earned."

She was definitely stiff-arming him. But he was the don't-quit king. "Give me the chance to earn it."

She pinched the bridge of her nose. He figured she must really not like him since it seemed to be such a huge decision to even be friends.

"Honestly, Abner. You're leaving. And I think it's better that way. I swore off men, and I don't think we can be friends."

"What about the friend you mentioned?" He tried to keep the heat out of his voice. Jealousy masquerading as anger.

She pursed her lips. "Bob? What about him?"

"He's your 'friend.'" He used air quotes. "You'd live with him."

A thought hit him. Hard enough to take a step backward.

Cora could live with him.

Only, no. He couldn't do that, exactly. Lots of people did it, and it might be fine for them, but his Amish roots would never allow him to do that.

Visiting was one thing. But if she were going to share his home, he'd want there to be rings and vows.

He almost snorted. He couldn't even get her to say he could be her friend. It would be hard to be any further from rings and vows.

But he was nothing if not determined.

"That's different," she finally said.

"How?" he shot back.

"It just is."

"Cora," he said, stepping a little closer, wanting so bad to touch her, but careful to give her space. "I was wrong. I made the coward's choice, thinking I was being virtuous. Give me as much of a chance as you're giving Bob."

"You're leaving."

If he knew her better, he might have said she was pushing him away in self-defense. That she was telling him no because she wanted him more than she wanted anyone else. But he didn't know and couldn't say.

"I'm staying until the end of the month. If that's okay with you." A decision he just made, although he'd told Doug he'd see that the house was closed up after she left.

He could spend Thanksgiving with Cora and her kids. The thought made him smile.

"What?" she asked suspiciously.

"I haven't eaten a Thanksgiving meal with a family since the Thanksgiving before my dad died." Yeah, he wasn't above pulling on her heartstrings.

"After all you've done for me, it would be an honor to have you here with us for Thanksgiving."

He felt a thrill of victory. He couldn't examine why it meant so much to him. Guilt wasn't the only thing that drove him. It was the only thing he could acknowledge.

She twisted her hands together, then finally dropped them and looked him in the eye. The moon was behind him, so he figured his face must be in shadow and maybe she couldn't see that his eyes were drawn to her lips. She definitely didn't know the fight he waged to keep his feet from moving closer, his hands from reaching out and touching the soft skin of her neck, and his lips from brushing her temple and moving lower.

"I don't think I can be friends with you." Her voice was husky and soft, and he almost would have said there was a bit of longing there, too, but that couldn't be, since she'd spent the last fifteen minutes rejecting him while he begged.

"Then give me two weeks to help you with the kids and fix the house up so Mom gets her security deposit back." Disappointment pulled down on his chest, but he didn't let it come out in his voice or expression. He wasn't the kind of man she wanted, anyway.

But she'd wanted him at one time. Maybe in two weeks, he could convince her to...to what? Wasn't there something wrong with him that he was mooning over a woman like Cora?

"I'd like to laugh with you some. We used to laugh a lot together." It hurt, he had to admit, that she didn't want to have anything to do with him, and his pride wanted him to shut his mouth about ten minutes ago, saddle up, and ride out. But he'd coddled his pride rather than listening to his heart, and that's what had gotten him into this position.

He could shove it aside. And focus his perseverance and never-quit attitude on changing Cora's mind. Regardless of how the rest of the world saw her, she was the only woman he'd ever wanted. He couldn't walk away without fighting for her. Not again.

At last, after long, never-ending minutes, she lifted a shoulder and spread her hand out. "I want you to stay. I'd like for you to. I just think it might be dangerous." She stepped around him. "I'm going to bed."

He fisted his hands rather than take her arm like he wanted to, pulling her to him, feeling her body next to his, tucking her head under his chin, and breathing in her scent.

He thought he knew what she meant by dangerous, and he had to agree. But he saw it as a good thing.

She was right. He could stay. He'd make the most of the opportunity.

Chapter 13

"I need the matches, Mom." Andrew stood in the kitchen doorway, his hands shoved in his jeans pockets, leaning his shoulder on the doorjamb. Just a few days and already her kids were imitating Abner in everything. From his speech to his expressions to the casual way he leaned in the doorway and followed her with hooded eyes.

"Please," Andrew added.

She bit back a grin. She'd just been about to correct him.

Walking to the cupboard for the requested item, she said, "What are you using them for?"

In the middle of summer, she might have allowed her children to go out and sit on the sidewalk and play with them—what was it going to hurt, short of setting themselves on fire, which, she had to admit, she assumed her kids had slightly more common sense than that. But it was fall, and there were leaves and sticks, and everything was dry. That'd be a nice exclamation point to the middle of her life—be responsible for the fire that burned the town down.

"Mr. Abner wants them."

She noted he didn't answer her question.

"For?" she asked again, holding the box of matches in one hand while cradling Claire, who grabbed at her hair, with the other.

"We been raking up leaves since we got home from school, and he said we could take the sticks and stuff that we got along with them and make a bonfire and roast marshmallows."

"I don't have any marshmallows." She felt a little bad about that. Abner had told her he'd take care of supper. She'd appreciated that since she'd put the babies down for naps and gotten started on the project she'd won the bid for. Claire and Luna had been up for a while now, but they'd been happy playing in the living room, and Cora had been able to keep working on her laptop. She'd only stopped about ten minutes ago.

"He walked to Martin's store and got them. He has hot dogs, too, and he said we'd eat supper around the fire tonight." Andrew's eyes sparkled.

Conflicting emotions warred in Cora's chest as she handed the matches over. Guilt was a big one. She'd never done anything like this with her kids. Fear. Her kids were going to fall in love with a man who was leaving. And, yeah. There was heat along with something softer and warmer that spread out from her heart and made her lips want to curl up and made her feet walk to the window so she could pull the curtain back.

The tall man in jeans and a ball cap, a flannel whose sleeves were rolled up to the elbows, helped Kohlton arrange a bunch of sticks in the fire pit that hadn't been in her yard when she woke up this morning. Luna squatted beside him, adorable in her purple coat and big pink hat. The leaves that had been spread all over her yard were in a pile beside the street, and the lawn was clean and neat. Even the weeds in the flower beds had been removed.

And sure enough, there was a package of marshmallows, sitting right beside two packages of hot dogs and rolls. Was that a package of chocolate bars under everything? She couldn't tell for sure, but it sure looked like it.

Her heart trembled in her chest, like the throat of an opera singer. How could she just be friends with that man? She wasn't even sure she could live in stony silence with him for the next two weeks and not fall completely in love with him.

If he'd asked her to be his girl, she'd have said yes in a heartbeat, unless she remembered in time that she needed to stand on her own. But every time he said "friends," it felt like her heart had hit a pincushion.

The light was fading, and soon they would need the glow from the fire Abner was now starting.

It wasn't hard to tell, though, that her kids were having a blast. Working. They'd cleaned the yard, weeded the flower beds, raked the leaves, and picked up sticks; even the little ones worked. But they were all smiles.

She couldn't begrudge her children this happiness.

There were no chairs, and she didn't have the folding camp chairs. The ground was damp and cold, and she hated to have them all sitting on it.

Putting a finger to her chin, she turned around. They could use towels.

Claire wiggled in her arms, and Cora adjusted her hold on the baby. She was getting hungry.

Her eyes landed on the kitchen table. Not even the table, but the chairs that surrounded it. Hey, why not?

Grabbing the back of one with the hand that wasn't holding Claire, she carried it down the hall and maneuvered it out the front door and down the porch steps.

"Hey, it's Mom!" Derrick yelled before he came running toward her when she appeared around the side of the house. He danced around the chair. "Can we bring more out?"

"You sure can," she said, smiling at his exuberance.

He took off running, Andrew and Summer close behind, laughing and excited that they were allowed to take the kitchen chairs outside.

"It's so easy to make children happy." Abner straightened and grinned down at her. Her heart turned over.

She ignored it and laughed. "Yeah. Kitchen chairs on the grass. Who would have thought that would be fun?"

His eyes, deep and blue, stared down at her, but she couldn't allow herself to get lost in a pair of eyes.

"They seemed to have fun being with you while you worked today, too."

"They were a help. The older boys especially once they got home from school. But even Kohlton's been carrying piles of sticks."

"I know. I saw him." She ran her nail over the back of her chair. "I know it's easier to do everything yourself rather than allow the kids, especially the little ones, to help." She tapped the chair with her finger before she looked up and met his gaze. She knew she couldn't be just friends with him, but she couldn't be ignorant, either. "Thank you so much for having the patience and putting up with them."

"Brings back good memories. It's been a fun day."

She couldn't read the expression on his face, but she thought he was sincere.

"You could have come out."

She shook her head. "I just wanted you to have chairs so you weren't sitting on the damp ground."

"Stay." His expression hadn't changed, but his tone held a note that sounded like pleading.

It had to be guilt he felt at knowing he'd judged her wrong. He wanted to be friends now to make it up to her.

She shook her head, turning to go back to the house.

Claire fussed, holding her hands out for Abner. Cora blinked and looked at her child. Really? Her daughter wanted Abner?

No. She couldn't leave him holding a baby that couldn't even walk. Without looking at him, she started toward the front porch.

Derrick, then Andrew, appeared around the side of the house, dragging kitchen chairs.

"You're not going back inside, are you?" Derrick asked, his face falling. Andrew, a little older, seemed to have a look on his face that said, "Of course she's not staying. She never does anything fun." Maybe it was her guilt that read that into it.

From around the corner, Summer cried, "Help me!"

Andrew left his chair and went back around, looking for his sister.

That sealed it for her. Andrew was such a good kid. And she wanted to be the mom he deserved. If that meant she had to go back to that fire and stand beside it, both literally and figuratively, she would. And she wouldn't allow herself to get burned. Abner wouldn't hurt her on purpose, anyway. But he couldn't help how she felt. That was on her.

She wasn't going to allow it to get in the way of making her children happy.

Picking up Andrew's chair, she said, "Come on, Derrick. I'll sit with you for a bit."

"Yes!" He did a fist pump and grabbed his chair, waddling with it to the fire. "I'm going back in and getting another."

"Me, too," Andrew said as he came up behind them, setting Summer's chair down and helping her up on it where she perched like a princess in front of her adoring subjects.

Cora had to grin at that. "You just need a crown, honey." She stroked the brown hair.

"I can help with that." Abner took some thin, supple sticks and worked for a few minutes twining them together in a circle.

His fingers were strong, looking more like they could run equipment and move cattle and stack hay bales and fix machinery than make a little girl a princess crown. Cora watched, the movement of his hands and fingers pulling her almost more than the brooding looks and wide shoulders. Not a physical attraction, but like strings of soft velvet were tugging her heart to his. Just from watching his hands.

She closed her eyes. If she couldn't resist the temptation, she needed to remove it.

Rustling came as he must have stood and moved to put the crown on Summer's head.

"Tired?" he said, low but loud enough to be heard over the chattering of her children.

Close her eyes, cut her ears off, and hold her nose. How could she remove temptation when it surrounded her?

"No." She opened her eyes and straightened her shoulders. She was a big girl, and she could do this.

She met his gaze before hers dropped to the crown in his hand. It looked a little big for Summer.

"Mom's first," Abner said, before he took another step closer and placed the crown on her head. If his fingers lingered a little longer than strictly necessary in her hair and if they seemed to stroke down a little on the soft strands, it was surely her imagination.

Claire reached for it immediately. Abner pulled a flat stone out of his pocket and held it out to her. "Saw this earlier. It was flat and looked a little like a heart. Maybe it would distract Claire from your crown."

Claire reached out, taking the rock in her chubby hands, saving Cora from the possibility of brushing his fingers.

But her eyes were drawn to his.

"What's that on your head, Mom?" Derrick said as he dragged another chair into position.

She looked away, grateful for the distraction. "Mr. Abner made me a crown."

He turned away, his movements somehow powerful and graceful at the same time. It wouldn't matter what he looked like, though. It was the kindness that he was showing to her children that was beating down her walls.

"Cool." Derrick was still young enough to love it. He jumped over the branches and wood that had been stacked next to the fire pit. "Will you make me one?"

"You can make your own. I'll show you how." Abner knelt by the pile and rooted through it.

"What about me?" Summer asked, still looking regal and glowing on her chair.

"I'm making yours now, sweetie. Do you want some pretty red berries on yours?"

"Yes!"

"You can't eat them."

Summer probably didn't need the warning, but it was Luna and Claire Cora worried about.

"It has to stay outside, and don't let your sisters have it, okay?" she said, anxiety making her words less warm and more sharp.

"Yep."

"How about a 'yes, ma'am,'" Cora said, not as sternly as she should have, because Summer looked adorable with her little chin jerking down in a nod and her toothpick arms crossed over her chest.

"Yes, ma'am," Summer said, with another nod.

"We'll just really have to watch that the little girls don't get those berries," Cora said to Abner, quietly, but he heard.

"Yes, ma'am," Abner said, tipping his ball cap, his eyes laughing.

"Stop your smarting off. There are plenty of sticks for me to choose from, and I'm not afraid to take you behind the woodshed."

"We have a woodshed?" Andrew asked, way too young to understand the subtext.

"If you want me to stop, that wasn't a good threat." Abner's lip pulled up, and she thought, she *thought*, he might be flirting with her.

Friends didn't flirt.

Which, of course, missed the larger point that men in general didn't flirt with a single mother of six children.

"Wasn't a threat. You'd better keep a civil tongue in your mouth, young man." She lifted her eyebrows and pursed her lips.

"I'll keep my tongue in my mouth. For now."

Cora couldn't help it. Her eyes got as big as they could go, and she glanced around at her children. Summer was still in her chair. Andrew and Derrick had abandoned their crown making and were wrestling on the ground. So much for the chairs to keep them off the dampness.

Kohlton ran around the yard with his arms out, apparently pretending to be an airplane, and Luna was still stuck to Abner's side.

They wouldn't get the insinuation. But none of them were paying attention. She'd had men around her children who hadn't been nearly so discreet. Their lack had been a real turnoff for her.

But Abner...he'd managed to heat her blood, shock her, and make her wonder if his words were just a threat. Or a promise.

But she couldn't quite get her sass level up to ask him.

Why not?

She lifted a brow. "Threat or promise?"

He straightened, scooping Luna up with him. His slow strides toward her somehow seemed threatening as her heart thudded with each step he took. He stopped in front of her and leaned down slightly.

How could a man with a little girl clinging to his neck with all her might be so entirely sexy and attractive?

Her heart skittered and flopped, and her lungs couldn't figure out whether they wanted to go in or out.

"It's not something I normally have a problem with. Been struggling now for a couple of days." His brow twitched. "It's a promise."

"Hey, look at this huge worm!" Andrew called out.

Both corners of Abner's lips curved up. "Frig. Let's hope 'worm' isn't code for 'snake.'"

She couldn't help it. She had to snort then laugh. So much easier to laugh because she just knew Abner would be taking care of it. Snake or worm, she didn't have to care.

The thought lifted about ten pounds off her shoulders.

As he moved away, saying, "Let's see it, boys," she caught a glimpse, and it truly was a worm. A granddaddy night crawler that was at least eight inches long. The biggest one she'd ever seen.

"We should take it fishing." Even Andrew couldn't keep from jumping up and down.

"If you want to catch a whale," Cora mumbled.

"Whales don't eat worms." Abner gave her a side-glance, his eyes glinting.

"Neither do fish. Not usually."

"The lady wins," he murmured.

"We can keep it as a pet," Derrick suggested.

"Not in my house," Cora said firmly. Wherever that was. She tossed that thought aside, unwilling to ruin the day.

"I dare you to eat it," Andrew said, with a cunning look only an older brother could achieve.

"Eww!" Derrick said.

"Scaredy-cat," Andrew taunted.

Abner stood back a little, watching, and didn't reprimand Andrew for taunting his brother. Cora opened her mouth to do it but closed it again. She didn't like to see it, but it wasn't hurting anything. Plus, she had the feeling Abner had everything under control.

"That's gross," Summer said.

"Go ahead, Derrick. Eat it."

"You eat it."

Andrew smiled. "What do I get if I eat it?"

"A fousand kisses from Mommy!" Kohlton yelled, like that was a great prize.

Andrew tilted his head, still young enough to think kisses from his mom were a good thing but probably trying to figure out if he wanted a thousand.

"Mom?" he asked. "You give out the prizes?"

"I'll give you two. But I don't think you should eat the worm."

"Why not?" Abner finally spoke, Luna still clasping his neck.

She wanted to ask him whose side he was on, but she probably didn't want to know the answer. She was the only one supporting the worm. It was a lonely team of two.

"Worms are actually really good for you. With that thought, Andrew, you probably ought not to eat that worm. Your mom'll have to buy you new shoes tomorrow, your feet will grow so fast."

Derrick had handed the worm to Andrew, and Andrew held it up to his face, moving his head this way and that as the worm wiggled and twisted in the air. "I don't think I want to eat it. Even for a thousand kisses."

"I'll do it for two," Abner said, his voice a lot softer than it had been and lacking the bluster that should have accompanied his words. His eyes were on the worm.

Cora's stomach felt like she'd just swallowed a bowling ball whole. Her fingers buzzed, and heat crept up her neck.

The kids erupted. "Yeah! We want to see you eat it!"

"Really? You'll eat it? That's so cool!"

Summer screamed, and even Kohlton stopped moving to stand and stare.

Cora knew her mouth was hanging open, but she couldn't seem to close it. Abner wasn't going to actually eat the worm, but she couldn't even believe he was joking about it. How was he going to get out of it? Did he expect her to intervene and stop him? Maybe she should start a save the worm chant. Something told her her kids would not join in. Maybe Claire would babble in baby talk with her.

Abner took the worm from a smirking Andrew.

Luna squealed and buried her head in his neck, gripping him tight with her arms and her legs.

"You want down, baby?" he asked her.

She squealed again, holding tighter.

He stood in profile to Cora. Her boys and Summer, who had finally gotten off her chair and tiptoed over, stood in front of him, watching, their eyes glued to the wiggling, shiny worm.

"It's dirty," Cora stated in the silence that had fallen on her little family.

"Dirt builds your immune system," Abner said easily.

"You're gonna have one hen of a germ killer in your body."

He just lifted a brow over sparkling eyes and looked at the boys. "Now, what exactly do I get for doing this?"

"A fousand kisses," Kohlton cried out.

"Two," Cora corrected automatically. The slow upturn of Abner's mouth into a full-toothed, wolfish grin was magnetic, and she couldn't rip her eyes away.

"I think a worm this big is worth more than two."

She wasn't sure where he'd learned to talk with that seductive undertone. Not the same place he'd learned to work with kids. The way his accent curled his words around her heart and the way the heat flashed in his eyes left her in no doubt that she was in serious trouble. *Serious* trouble.

"Yeah, Mom. Probably at least ten." Derrick put his hands on his hips, like the question merited serious consideration.

"That's a lot," she said, more for self-preservation than anything, because that worm was a monster, and if he truly ate it, he deserved his own TV show or something. Not that she could picture anyone but her bloodthirsty children wanting to watch it.

"Two kisses and I get to sit beside you while we eat." He glanced at the fire pit where the flames had died down. One of the kids had brought the hot dogs and rolls over, and they sat beside the stones he'd just laid down that day.

Cora's blood roared in her ears like a river at flood stage. Her chest rose and fell, and she couldn't find her words. Some sassy retort to let him know that she was fine. She wasn't, of course, but she could fake it in front of her kids.

Only she really couldn't.

"Come on, Mom. That's not hard. You can do it."

"I'll sit on the other side of you and hold your hand," Derrick offered gallantly.

"Yeah," she finally breathed out. "Because if he eats that worm, I think I'm gonna be afraid of him. I'm not sure I want to kiss him, either."

That statement made Abner's grin get wider. "You can kiss me first."

"That's not fair. You have to eat the worm first." Andrew seemed concerned that the worm might not get eaten.

Cora kind of regretted she hadn't been more of an animal rights person and passed that trait on to her children. "Are worms endangered?" she asked as a last-ditch effort to stall the execution and, hence, the kissing.

Her boys' faces scrunched up. "Huh?"

Abner snorted. "Think not."

"I don't know why you're smiling," she snapped. "You're the one that has to eat it."

"Reward's worth it," he said in that same voice that curled her toes.

She grabbed the end of her ponytail and twisted. Finding her sass, she tossed her head. "Go ahead, then. I'm watching."

"Thought you were going to close your eyes?"

"Someone has to make sure the worm actually makes it to the designated destination. I wouldn't want you to receive rewards you haven't earned."

"I wouldn't want to take anything that you don't want to give," he said, serious, and she thought he was giving her an out. She sure didn't want it, but she didn't want to admit it, either.

"If you earn it, you'll get it." Her fingers squeezed the hair that was wrapped around them.

A small curve bent his lip. "I'd do something a lot harder than this to earn a prize like that."

Before she could respond, he looked around at the kids. "Ready, guys?"

A chorus of "yeahs" rang out.

He lifted the worm up. Cora truly did want to close her eyes. The wiggling worm with a few pieces of dirt still stuck to it made her want to hold her stomach and lean over.

Abner dropped it in his mouth and closed, chewing, holding his hands out, like that proved he wasn't doing something nefarious with the worm in his mouth.

Just thinking of the wiggling and the squishing and the...*ugh*, going on in his mouth made bile back up in Cora's throat, and her stomach curled into a little ball and tried to sneak out her backbone.

About twenty seconds later, Abner swallowed and opened his mouth, pointing it at the boys.

"It's gone," Andrew said, his lips barely moving and his eyes looking like he'd just looked into a fresh tomb. Which, strictly speaking, he had.

"You really ate it," Derrick said, in that same hushed, shocked tone.

Summer stared at his mouth. Then her eyes moved to his face. Cora really couldn't tell if she was appalled or amazed. Maybe both. Or, since she was five, probably more amazed than appalled.

"I did." Abner shrugged. "They're actually kinda good for you, but they taste like wet socks that have been left in a basement for a year."

"I don't think I could have handled the wiggling," Cora said, still not sure her stomach had reattached itself into its proper position. Seemed like it might have been sitting on the front steps waiting on a taxi. Maybe a neighbor would take pity and call an Uber.

"Just makes it more challenging." With one more look at the boys, opening his mouth and hands, he picked up a chair and moved it over beside Cora. "My seat."

She raised her brows, not sure how she felt about the whole worm deal but entirely too sure on how she felt about Abner.

Chapter 14

"If I give you my knife, will you sharpen some sticks for us?" Abner asked. Cora still looked a little grossed out, and he hoped it wasn't a permanent feeling for her. That wasn't the first worm he'd ever eaten, although, he had to say, it was easily the biggest.

Still, he meant every word when he said he'd do something a lot harder to win that prize.

"Mom has to kiss you," Derrick said, picking out a stick from the pile.

"Maybe we'd better wait until her stomach has settled a little," Abner suggested. He'd prefer she wasn't green and looking like she was going to throw up when she kissed him for the first time. From the way she was acting, it would probably be a peck on the forehead, but wherever her lips landed, he was going to enjoy it.

"Sometimes she forgets. Don't let her," Andrew warned.

"Maybe after we eat," Abner said, pulling his pocketknife out. "I'll take Claire."

"I was going to go in and get her highchair. It might as well be out here with the rest of the kitchen furniture," Cora said matter-of-factly.

"If all the furniture ends up out here, are we going to move the bonfire into the kitchen?"

"That might be a little hard to explain to the landlord."

"That we burnt the house down? Yeah." Abner grinned. "'Course, Thanksgiving dinner around a campfire might be more 'traditional' than around a table."

"The pilgrims worked hard so we don't have to," Cora replied.

"Nothing wrong with hard work."

"Nothing wrong with modern conveniences. Like a house."

"Well, boys. Guess your mother wants to be boring and eat Thanksgiving inside," Abner said lightly, thinking she wouldn't take offense but take it like the teasing he meant it to be.

"Like the rest of the country." She rolled her eyes.

Yeah, she could take teasing.

"Aw, Mom," Derrick whined.

"We could eat outside for the rest of our lives." Andrew looked hopefully at Abner. A sharp pinch gripped his chest, because he hadn't been given the choice to stay.

"That would get old, then it would be a treat to eat inside," Cora said reasonably, taking the knife he handed her, while he took Claire off her shoulder.

"But for Thanksgiving. That would be fun!" Derrick slapped Andrew's upraised hand and they jumped around together.

"We've never done that before." Summer looked a little skeptical.

"Could we really do it, Mr. Abner?" Andrew stopped and looked at Abner like he could actually make that decision.

Abner shrugged. "It's up to your mom."

Cora snorted. "If you want to try to cook a turkey over an open fire, you have right at that thing. I'm fine with it. I'll take a morning nap and get up in time to belly up to the...campfire."

"Guess that's a no. I'm not doing it without your mother." Abner shrugged.

"Oh, no. I'm not going to be the bad guy in this situation. You're the one who suggested cooking Thanksgiving over the campfire. Own it, mister."

"I am owning it. With you." His grin got a little crafty. "Haven't you ever heard the borrower is servant to the lender?"

"I have, but I have no idea what that has to do with anything, other than I suspected you were slightly nuts when you ate that worm, and now I'm convinced you'd have to go backward to park there."

"What does that mean about servants?" Summer asked.

"It means, honey," Abner said, "that people who owe things are servants to the people who don't. Which, since your mother owes me two kisses, she's my servant."

Cora's mouth dropped. She didn't seem to be able to decide whether to be offended or to laugh. "Talk about taking the Bible and twisting it to suit your purposes. My children will be warped for life."

"You're telling me you don't owe me?" he asked, putting a hot dog on the stick that Cora had made for Summer and keeping an eye on the boys as they held their hot dogs over the fire. "Or are you saying you're gonna renege?"

"I would never." Her eyes flashed. "I have no idea what that has to do with anything, anyway. Your argument isn't going in a straight line."

"It was easy to follow. You're cooking Thanksgiving dinner with me. Out here. The kids will help. It'll be fun."

"And I have to help you why?"

"Because you owe me."

She stood up. He grinned. Supper just got a lot more interesting.

"That's it. I don't care if you just ate a worm. I'm paying you now, because I can't stand to have you lord it over my head for one more second."

He stood still, Claire in one arm, Luna hugging his leg, as Cora stomped across the six feet that separated them.

Man, she was beautiful. Maybe not in a classic sense where she'd be a cover model or a pinup. But with the fire and fun in her eye and the way she moved and the fun he had dancing with their words. He'd rather hold her and dance for real, but she'd take his teasing and give it back, gently or with a kick. Either way, she held his heart.

He waited while she stopped in front of him. Unless she was going to plant one on his collarbone and make it count, or jump up and slap one on the bottom of his chin, she wasn't paying her bet off yet. He was planning a kiss that would need a "13" after the PG.

He smirked at her as realization dawned over her face that she'd need his help in order to pay her bet.

Her chin jutted out.

He started speaking before she could. "We could compromise."

Her eyes narrowed.

"I need a roll." Derrick came over with a hot dog that was black on one side and looked to be cold on the other. It would probably taste better than a worm, but not by much. The nutrition value would come in second, though. A hot dog was definitely not whole food. A worm, on the other hand...

Cora pursed her lips before bending and picking up the bag of rolls at her feet. He waited, making sure Summer was okay with her hot dog and Kohlton still hadn't decided to cook one. Luna was still beside him, and Claire seemed happy in his arms.

Cora stood again, her hands on her hips, a sharpened stick she'd gotten from somewhere in her hands.

He eyed it. "Wanna trade?" He jiggled Claire.

"No." She smiled sweetly. Then she put the hot dog in her hand on the stick and held it out over the fire, bringing Kohlton into her arm. "What was your compromise?"

"We'll eat dinner inside and cook dessert outside."

"Pumpkin pies over the fire?" She gave him a doubtful look.

"Mountain pies."

"Well, that actually sounds nice, but I don't have any mountain pie makers."

"Oh, woman of little faith."

She grinned. Maybe she'd had as bad of a childhood as he had, but she'd been in church enough to get his Bible references.

"We have three days. I think the boys and I can figure something out."

"Yeah, we can do it!" Andrew shouted.

"Do what?" Derrick asked.

Andrew shrugged.

Cora bit back a smile. "Are you going to bend down here so I can pay you?"

Abner lifted his brows. "Half now, half later?"

Cora sighed. "Okay."

"I want the big half later." He pitched his voice low and smiled when she shivered.

"Guess you flunked math." She flipped her ponytail over her shoulder and helped Kohlton to hold the stick.

He affected a wounded air. "I offer a compromise, I'm gonna bend down and accommodate the short woman—"

She gasped and put her hands on her hips, almost losing Kohlton's hot dog.

He ignored her and went on, "And how does she pay me back, except insult my intelligence."

"Halves, by definition, are equal."

He smiled, shaking his head. "Let me put it to you this way." He looked over, seeing that Andrew and Derrick had finished their hot dogs and were helping Summer put hers in a roll. Lowering his voice, he said, "I'll take a kiss the kids can see now. But I want the other one after they go to bed."

His eyes glinted into hers.

Her mouth opened. Then closed. She caught her lip between her teeth, and something like fear pinched her eyes.

It hurt that she didn't seem to want him. And maybe the harder he chased her, the faster she would run, but he didn't have time to back off. He only had two weeks. Less than.

So he didn't let up, and he didn't back off.

Her lips weren't smiling. Her voice was little more than a whisper. It didn't have to be loud. They were standing right in front of each other. "Just because I have six kids doesn't mean I'm easy."

Oh, that hurt, and he closed his eyes, backing up after all. How could the words that came from his heart and out his mouth hit her so much differently than how he meant them to?

"Maybe at one time, that was true," she said.

These words hurt worse.

"But it's not anymore." She bent down, helping Kohlton take his hot dog out of the fire and getting him a roll.

She placed Kohlton on a chair, and he was standing beside her, ready, when she stood up. "I never said you were. I never thought you were. Not for me."

"Your mother just left, and you're already talking about what we're going to do when the kids go to bed. I'm out." She hadn't raised her eyes to meet his, and she turned.

He caught her arm. Not demanding but asking her to stop.

She did. But she didn't look at him.

"I'll sit on my hands if it will make you feel better. But I kinda wanted to touch you the first time I kissed you. Been waiting for it for years."

Her eyes shot to his.

He couldn't tell if she'd figured out what he was saying. He supposed it didn't matter. It wasn't like he could prove it. She'd have to take his word for it, although he wasn't in the habit of lying. Again, not something she'd know.

"Thought you said you wanted to be 'friends?'" Her eyes held derision, and he knew, again, she hadn't understood.

"I do."

"With benefits?" Her eyes narrowed. "No thank you."

"Can I have another hot dog?" Summer asked, blinking up from beside them.

"Of course you can, sweetie," Cora said, moving away and grabbing the package.

Kohlton needed help, and he balanced Claire in one arm while putting the hot dog that Kohlton must have gotten out himself on the stick. He doubted the boy would eat a second one, but it was possible. Working in the cool fall air could really stir up an appetite.

By the time he was done, Andrew had burned two marshmallows black and wanted Abner to show him how to cook them and Cora had Luna up on her lap and used his knife to cut up pieces of a hot dog to feed her.

He wanted to tease her about falling in love with his knife, but after the way their conversation had ended, he wasn't sure she was even talking to him.

Dang it. He liked her. Maybe more. He'd already fallen for her kids. He wanted this to be his life. He'd be happy to spend every day like this, hanging out in the backyard, flirting with his girl, loving on his kids, but anticipating bedtime. They just needed a dog to eat the hot dogs that fell on the ground and about six more kids. And a North Dakota sky. The Ohio sky might be the same in theory, but in reality, it wasn't wild enough for him.

Maybe he just wasn't made to live in town. He'd do it, though, if he got everything else he wanted. It wasn't just any family. He wanted this one. And there was only one girl that would do. Man, he didn't know what he would do if she wouldn't take him this time.

The stars were out in force, and the fire had died down. Cora had made a lot of s'mores for the kids, and he held two sleepy little girls in his arms. He was pretty sure he had chocolate on his face and neck and melted marshmallow stuck in his beard. If he were going to stay here for the next ten days or so, he'd need to go to town and buy a razor.

He'd never gotten to sit in the seat beside Cora, but facing her across the fire was almost as nice.

Derrick and Andrew had quit wrestling and lay stretched out, looking at the stars. Cora held Kohlton, and Summer sat at her feet. He supposed they should have brought a book out and read some. If he remembered correctly, Cora had a pretty nice singing voice as well.

It had been a good day and a great evening. He was tired, pleasantly so, from physical labor and from having fun with his family.

"It's bedtime." Cora stood. The boys groaned, but they got up, too. She carried Kohlton and held her hand out for Summer.

Abner stood. The fire was glowing embers and nothing more. "I'll take care of putting those out completely, but I'll help you get the kids upstairs first."

"Thanks," she said, and he assumed he wasn't getting the silent treatment.

"You boys can each carry a chair in. I'll get the rest of them." It wouldn't take long to carry the chairs in, but it wouldn't hurt the boys to help.

"Make sure there's no dirt stuck to the bottoms of them," Cora instructed.

It took about twenty minutes to get the kids wiped down and teeth brushed and ready for bed. Abner had changed Claire and handed her off to Cora, who acted like she didn't see him. Maybe she was thinking about paying the bet off, or maybe she was still miffed because she thought he'd wanted more than she had offered.

He slipped downstairs, wanting to stay but feeling like Cora didn't want him to. It wasn't his family.

He doused the burning embers with water and carried the last two chairs into the kitchen. Cora stood at the sink, wringing her hands before dropping them to her sides.

The way she was acting, he kinda felt like she was going to give him his walking papers. He didn't think he could fight her to stay. He'd pushed as hard as he dared tonight, and she'd been pretty clear about her no. If she told him to pack it up, what other choice did he have?

He set the chair down and stood in front of her with a good six feet between them and braced himself. If she wouldn't walk with him, he'd walk alone. He could be in North Dakota by midnight tomorrow. And miserable for the rest of his life.

"Are you going to sit down?" she asked.

"Are you?"

"After you do."

That was odd. But he sat, nerves twisting and balling and pulling in his stomach. He tried to remember to breathe.

Cora, unsmiling, walked slowly over. She didn't stop, as he expected her to, and didn't take a chair of her own, but continued until she was beside him, bending down and touching her lips to his forehead. They stayed there, it felt like forever but not long enough, and he closed his eyes, breathing in all the scents that mixed together, the chocolate and marshmallow, the hot dogs and woodsmoke, little kids and, under it all, that totally unique, slightly sweet, and very evocative scent that was all Cora. The one that used to be overlaid with cotton candy but had matured along with the girl into a womanly scent that made him feel like he'd do anything, anything at all, to keep the woman it belonged to.

She straightened and didn't speak until he opened his eyes. It took him a minute.

"That was one."

He nodded, because he couldn't talk.

"Sit on your hands."

His lungs froze, and his mouth went dry. He was thankful to be sitting down, too. But she still wasn't smiling, and he hadn't changed his mind about taking what she didn't want to give.

"You don't have to do this."

Her eye twitched. "I want to."

He wasn't sure he believed her. She didn't look happy about it. He stared into her eyes. There was determination there. Something else, but he wasn't sure what it was.

"Sit on them," she repeated.

His jaw tightened. He wanted this. Wanted it more than he wanted to see the sun come up tomorrow.

If he sat on his hands, it would be her making all the decisions. He didn't want to give up that control, but he'd said he would, and he had to believe it was worth it.

He moved slowly, putting his hands flat on the seat under his butt. She waited.

"That's where they stay."

He jerked his head up, not trusting his voice.

She narrowed one eye as though sizing him up, started to move to one side, then the other. Finally, she tilted her head and lifted a shoulder like she was giving up. But she moved in front of him and put both hands on his shoulders.

She straddled his legs and put her butt down on the end of his knees. Primly.

It made him smile.

She wrinkled her forehead.

He forced his lips down. He looked at her from under hooded eyes. They just wouldn't stay up. But he wanted to see her, because she was the only girl he'd ever want to do this with.

"I'm not going to kiss you if you're going to laugh at me," she whispered.

"I can guarantee you I'm not laughing."

His words were heartfelt and sincere, but her lips flattened like she didn't like them. He'd never practiced words that would win a woman's heart, and he wasn't sure how to start now. She didn't want to hear what he wanted to tell her.

She leaned forward and tilted her head. He watched her come, feeling like it could be a dream.

He'd eaten the darn worm, and this was what he wanted, but the nagging feeling that she was only paying a debt took away the pleasure he wanted to share.

"Stop, please," he whispered. His voice was hoarse and rough, as he knew it would be.

Her face was close, her lips just a whisper away from his. Their breath mingled.

"What?" she asked softly, her brows crinkled.

Her weight on his legs and shoulders felt right and good, and she was almost as close as he wanted her, but... "You don't want this. And I don't want it if you don't want it." His heart hurt, his chest burned, but it was the truth.

Her eyes searched his. "What makes you think I don't want it?" she asked, her voice still soft.

How could he tell her what he'd read on her face? He asked instead, "Do you?"

Her hands came up and cupped his face, sliding against the stubble that had turned into a beard. "Abner."

The touch of her hand was everything he'd dreamed it would be, and he closed his eyes, wanting to pull his own hands out and slide them down her back, pulling her close, tucking her into his body, and holding her tight.

Then, soft as a prayer at midnight, her lips touched his.

His eyes flew open. They closed almost immediately, and he groaned, wanting to press forward, wanting more, but knowing, in some small corner of his mind, he'd given that to her to decide.

She pressed into him lightly, her fingernails grazing the sensitive skin below his ear, and he gave under her pressure.

Torture. This is what he'd eaten the worm for, to sit under this sweet torture. Hot as lava, cold as the Titanic's grave, he could hardly stand it and never wanted it to end.

He couldn't say how long it was until she pulled back, looking far less assured than she had when she sat down.

He didn't have words, and she didn't say anything either, but got up and slipped by him. A few moments later, he heard her footsteps on the stairs, then the kitchen was quiet except for the pounding of his heart and the harshness of his breath.

Chapter 15

The week flew past.

Abner didn't seem to want to talk about the kiss, and Cora didn't know what to say, so she didn't say anything.

She'd kissed her share of men, and had been kissed in return, but she'd never felt like *that* before. She couldn't even describe it, so she didn't. Just pretended it didn't happen. He'd wanted to be friends. That kiss proved to her that she'd been right. She couldn't just be friends.

Abner didn't bring it up, and they fell into a routine. Kids off to school in the morning. She took care of the little ones until lunch. After that, the kids went down for a nap and she worked. He made supper. She supervised the homework, if any, and he played with the kids until bedtime.

They had time off school for Thanksgiving and hunting season. Abner didn't seem to be a hunter; at least, he didn't act like he was missing anything when he took the boys outside and worked on fixing the loose siding, replacing the gutter that had fallen down, and building a whole new set of steps and railing for the porch.

That's just what she saw. Maybe they did more. The boys came in tired at night anyway.

A couple of times, she wanted to ask Abner if he had a job, since he didn't seem concerned about getting back to anything and he was never on his phone.

Thanksgiving had come and gone. Abner and the boys had pieced together something to make mountain pies with, and the campfire in the backyard had brought back a lot of memories for her while her children had made new ones.

It was the best Thanksgiving she could remember.

Abner helped her get the kids upstairs and washed up, but he slipped away while she was tucking them in. Maybe to take care of the fire.

He'd been so good to them, not just today, but since he'd come and she just wanted to make sure she thanked him.

Plus, she had kind of been getting the idea that he might be feeling a little melancholy maybe, and she wanted to talk to him.

But he wasn't downstairs when she went back down ten minutes later, although the chairs were all back around the kitchen table.

So she put a jacket on and walked outside and around the side of the house where the fire pit was.

She didn't see him at first, but the fire still glowed red and she moseyed over, smiling a little at the memories they'd made around it in the last week.

She hadn't wanted to be dependent on any man, and she still didn't, but she could admit that Abner made things fun.

It was not quite as easy to admit that she sought him out because she wanted to be with him.

"Hey."

His voice came from the oak beside the fence and she strained to see, finally walking a few feet beyond the burning embers and then able to make out his outline sitting at the base of the tree, leaning against it.

"Mind if I join you?" she asked.

"Love it." He didn't hesitate, although his voice was low and sounded a little sad.

She sat a quarter of the way around the tree, with her back to it. It wasn't a massive trunk, and she could still reach behind her and touch him, although she didn't.

They sat in silence for a while. Low clouds racing across the moon and the wind rattling branches and causing the leaves that hadn't yet fallen to make a sandy, rustling sound. A car went by down the block on the main street and on the other side of town a dog barked.

Cora twisted her fingers in her lap. She'd wanted to thank him, but when she spoke, that wasn't what she said.

"You've been here over a week, yet you haven't gone to see your Amish family. Why not?"

She was prying. She hadn't meant to, but that was a question that had been popping up in her mind.

The wind swept her words away.

Knowing that it must be a hard subject for him, but unwilling to let it go yet, she spoke gently. "When we dated before, you'd mentioned that your dad and a brother had died and you'd gone to live with your real mom. I got the feeling there was more to the story."

He blew out a slow breath, then spoke slowly. "There is."

"You don't have to tell me, of course. You're just so good with the kids, and you've been amazing with us and I wanted to thank you. I just also thought you probably have a real family who'd like to see you."

"No. They don't want to see me."

"That can't be true."

"I killed my dad and brother."

She gasped and straightened, a little spiral of fear twisting in her chest and pinching her stomach. But it was Abner, and immediately she knew there was more to the story. She leaned back against the tree, the rough bark cutting through her coat.

"I know that isn't what it sounds like," she said matter-of-factly.

"Yeah. I was on the roof and my dat and brother were standing below. Dat was explaining something to my brother and he handed up a piece of metal to me. I wasn't ready for it – I'd taken my glove off for some reason. The edge sliced my hand when I went to grab for it. I'd have died rather than let go, but the blood made it slippery and...I just couldn't hold it." He blew out a breath and moved like he just couldn't sit still. "Know how many times I've relived that moment? Wished I could have squeezed tighter with my hand? Or flipped the piece of metal up somehow?" He swallowed and the sound felt loud and agonized in the darkness. "Just wish I could redo. I would jump off the roof before I'd let it slip out of my hand again."

There was silence for a bit before he finished in a low voice. "Hit them both in the neck. Got the people in the house to call, but... no details, just neither one made it more than a couple of minutes."

"Oh, wow. That's awful." Her stomach had jerked into a quivering ball. It wasn't hard to imagine what the sharp side of a piece of metal would do to the flesh of a man's neck.

"You didn't do it on purpose. Couldn't your mother forgive you?"

"She wasn't my mother." He shifted and she turned to see him peering at her in the dark.

"My father slept with my birth mother not long before he married his Amish wife. Then he brought me home to live with them just a few months before my brother was born. If I were mamm, I wouldn't like me either."

Maybe that explained why he'd always worked so hard back when they were in school. She'd heard rumors that he'd do anything and never complain. She'd always figured he was raised that way, but maybe he'd started out trying to earn his mother's favor. What child doesn't want their mother to love them?

She pulled her lips in between her teeth, hurting for the child he'd been.

"I can see pity on your face, and I don't need it. I'm just telling you why they don't want to see me."

"What about your siblings?"

"Saw a brother at the hardware store. We talked. They're doing good. They know I'm doing good. He said they don't hold any hard feelings, but..." He sighed. "I guess it's hard to explain, but I don't belong there. Don't belong with my English family. Just...don't belong."

She moved her hand over until it touched his and her fingers slid over his knuckles and twined with his fingers. "You made me feel like I had a real family today. Like I hadn't screwed my life up and my kids were paying for it. It felt like a true holiday, one that belonged on the Hallmark channel." She laughed a little, because she was way too screwed up to be on the Hallmark channel, but it hadn't felt that way today. "I really just came out here to thank you."

His fingers tightened on hers. "I should be the one thanking you. Being here, with you, and your children, you guys make me feel like I belong. Finally."

He didn't say anything more and neither did she.

Eventually the embers burned out and they walked in together, separating when she went up the stairs to her room, and he walked down the hall. The sadness that had seemed to be a part of him after the kids went to bed was gone, but there was some kind of lingering tightness in her chest. She wasn't sure exactly what it was, but she had spent almost a full day not worried about the future.

So, therefore she made some phone calls on Friday and a large white van pulled up to her house Saturday morning while they were all still at the breakfast table.

"Did someone just stop along the street?" Andrew asked, his head tilted. He pushed away from the table.

"No." Cora gave Claire a bite of egg and stood, glancing at Abner who was feeding Luna and didn't seem the slightest bit concerned about any potential company. "I'll check. You eat."

He did glance up at that, his brows a little furrowed, but he definitely didn't suspect what she had done.

Hopefully it wasn't a disaster.

By the time she reached the front door and opened it, three ladies in bonnets and black dresses with white aprons had gotten out of the van. Four men in black pants with straw hats stood with them, looking at the house.

Cora closed the front door behind her and stepped off the porch, walking toward the group, holding her hand out.

"I'm Cora," she said to the man who'd moved the closest to the gate.

"Eli," he said. "I got your message and although Mamm wouldn't come, the seven of us siblings wanted to."

"Thank you," she said, not sure if she'd ever meant anything more. "He's in the house and he doesn't have any idea that I even called you or that you're here." She hadn't wanted them to refuse to come and hadn't been sure they would. Communication wasn't easy, since none of them lived with phones in their house and they weren't allowed answer machines. It would have hurt Abner more to know that they'd been asked to visit and refused.

She led the way down the path, through the door and into the kitchen.

Abner glanced up as she walked into the bright light. He did a double take, rising immediately, lines between his brows.

Cora's heart shivered. He didn't look happy.

"Iddo?" Abner said. "Eli?"

The Amishmen smiled, their hats in their hands. "It's us," Eli said. "Along with John, Paul, Nancy, Mary and Sally. Anna May moved to Lancaster, Pennsylvania when she married and couldn't come. But she wanted to be here."

"Mamm?" Abner almost whispered.

Eli shook his head. "I don't think she's holding onto any grudges, but she didn't want to open up all the bad memories, either."

Abner moved, then, around the table, holding his hand out to shake with his brothers, but they didn't let him off with a handshake, each of them grabbing him in a bear hug that involved a lot of back slapping. Abner didn't even try to shake with his sisters, but hugged them too.

Cora cooked chili for lunch and Abner's siblings were still talking to him when she put her children down for their naps.

She had a glow in her heart at the joy that lit Abner's face. It was too bad his mother hadn't seen fit to come, but probably knowing that none of his siblings harbored any ill will toward him healed his heart as much as anything could.

They left several hours before supper. Abner saw them out and came straight back in the house, going straight to Cora where she sat on the floor playing blocks with Claire.

He knelt down beside her. "Thank you for calling them and inviting them to come." He put his hand on her arm.

She looked at it before she met his eyes, serious as she'd ever seen them. How could she tell him she was just happy to maybe repay just a little of what he'd done for her? How could she let him know that the debt she owed him was so much bigger than a phone call and invite?

So, she didn't. She just smiled and said, "You're welcome."

All the cares and worries that she had somehow disappeared in the peace and contentment that radiated out from him before he moved away, taking the boys outside to fix the loose siding before supper.

The days slipped by and Sunday dawned, cool and cloudy. Cora had two more days before she had to move and not a clue where she was going. It would have helped if more than one of the jobs she'd applied for online had come through. Working independently was nice for flexibility, but she needed a steady paycheck.

Abner carried Luna who had bonded to him so strongly Cora almost wished he'd never come. Luna was going to be devastated when he left.

She carried Claire, and the other kids were scattered between and beside them. Like they were a real family walking to church. Odd, really. Since as far as she knew he was only there because he'd told Doug he'd stay and close up the house after Cora left.

He'd been working hard on fixing it and letting her boys help, which made them feel capable and necessary.

They stepped into the church, and the scent of wood and Bibles and hymnbooks mixed with the newer scent of pine sap as the windowsills were filled with greenery.

Cora followed Abner and the children to an empty pew, and she relaxed, soaking up the spirit-soothing atmosphere.

But a sadness tugged at the back of her mind, and she fought melancholy.

This was her last Sunday here. The preacher asked for volunteers to decorate the greenery that had been put around, and the Christmas season schedule was announced, and she couldn't participate in any of it.

She wanted to put down roots. Wanted to move somewhere and stay there for the rest of her life. Wanted to raise her children in a solid environment.

And yet, here she was, moving once again. There'd been a definite yes on one of the apartments she applied for, but it was the worst out of everything she'd applied to, and she didn't want to move her kids there, but felt she had no choice.

The moving van was coming tomorrow to get Aunt Sandy's stuff.

Yeah, the whole situation just made her exceptionally sad.

They walked down after church and had sandwiches for lunch. Abner touched her arm as she herded the youngest four up the stairs for a nap.

She stopped, surprised. They'd not said much of anything to each other since she'd kissed him. It'd been so long, she decided he must have hated it.

"Are you okay?" he asked, lines appearing between his brows.

She nodded. She'd not expected him to notice.

"I have the boys," he said.

She figured as much but didn't say anything, answering with another nod.

He held on just a few seconds longer. She didn't wait for him to let go, but shifted Claire in her arms and moved after her children.

She put all the kids in their own beds. Sometimes, if she wasn't working, she'd just let them snuggle with her, but even though she'd finished another job and had that money in her account, the future seemed so uncertain that she could hardly stand it. She had six little people depending on her, and she didn't know what to do.

Lying down on the bed that wouldn't be there tomorrow after the movers came, she kept still until Claire snored softly in her play yard that doubled as a crib.

She knew everything would be okay. Even though she'd made a lot of mistakes, God was still with her and would work things out. She just wasn't sure how.

The lack of roots and the vagabond lifestyle was all her fault, but she hated that her children would suffer.

And of course, they'd miss Abner.

A tear slipped out of her closed eye and down her cheek. Followed by another. And another. Tears, but no sound. She didn't want to wake Claire.

A small noise by the door caused her eyes to fly open.

Abner stood in the doorway. He'd helped put the kids to bed most nights but otherwise had not been upstairs.

His eyes went to the baby in the crib. He didn't make a sound as he walked across the floor, sat on the bed, and lay down beside her, not hesitating, like that was their normal.

She noted he was in his stocking feet.

She also noted that the bed felt a lot smaller with him in it.

"I have something I've been wanting to ask you. Couple things."

He had to have seen her tears, but she was grateful he didn't comment on them. She wasn't sure why she was crying. She certainly couldn't explain it to him.

"I'm listening." She could feel the heat coming off him, remembered their kiss, and wished she could have been what he wanted.

"Do you know what you're doing?"

She didn't figure there was any reason for her to pretend to not know what he was talking about. Much as she didn't want to admit how sad her life was.

"I have an apartment in Huntingdon, which is just about an hour north of here."

"Yeah, I know where it is."

She'd forgotten he'd grown up in the area, too. Of course he knew where Huntingdon was.

"I have a moving van scheduled to come the day after tomorrow. I'll be driving down the same time as them and getting the keys."

"You've already paid a deposit?"

"Yes. I put a deposit to hold it, and I'll owe more when I get there."

Out of the corner of her eye, she could see his chest go up and down. She supposed his presence should make her nervous, but it had the opposite effect.

"What are your plans?" she asked, after he didn't say anything for a while.

"I have a ranch in North Dakota. Just bought it from a buddy of mine. Makes this house look like a castle."

Wow. It must be pretty run-down and tiny.

"Is Huntingdon where you want to be?" he asked, a little softer.

"No." She didn't elaborate.

"Thought maybe you'd want to raise the kids in the country and not an apartment."

"Of course that's what I want. But it's not what I get." She tried to shake the irritation out of her voice. "Which is fine. The kids will be fine."

"You could have that."

"Sure if I won the lottery. But since I don't play..." She raised a hand and waved it, then dropped it back on her stomach.

He took a deep breath. If it had been anyone else but Abner, she'd have thought he was nervous.

"You could come to North Dakota with me." His head turned, and his eyes searched her face. Rolling over on his side, he touched a finger to her face. His lips flattened and pulled back. "This hurts my heart."

She closed her eyes and turned away. She was pretty sure he was asking her to live with him. It wasn't hard to figure out what he wanted. She wanted it too, but Abner would put a ring on the finger of the girl he loved. Since he wasn't, he was basically offering her a home, and not a very good one from the sounds of it, for her children and herself in exchange for...

His finger trailed down her cheek and into her hair. "I watch you play with this, and my fingers itch to touch it."

"I thought you were better than that." Her head turned back toward him. She couldn't keep the hurt out of her eyes. So what if he knew?

His brows crinkled. "Better than what?"

She lowered her voice so she didn't wake Claire. "Never mind." She couldn't hardly fault him when she'd done all that and worse. She'd just expected more from him. Maybe she should have expected it from herself.

"I don't know what you're talking about." There was a pleading note in his voice.

"Nothing." She sighed. She'd disappointed a lot of people, too. "I told myself I wasn't depending on a man again."

"I know. That's why I've hesitated so long. I know you don't...want a man. I get it. So, how about you come with me until you get on your feet? Maybe you'll decide to stay, and maybe something better will come along."

She wanted to. Her kids loved Abner. And so did she. How could she not?

"Just one thing," he said.

Yeah. This was where he said she'd have to sleep with him in order to get what she wanted. She promised herself, no matter how much she loved him, she'd tell him no. She formed the word in her mouth and put it on the edge of her tongue.

"Marry me."

She choked, lifting her head off the bed. "What?"

He blew his breath out. "Marry me. We don't have to...share a bed, I just can't stay in the same house..." His voice trailed off.

He'd shocked her. Truly.

"I thought you said I was free to go?"

"You are. Would be. I know people live together all the time. You've done it." He paused. "But I can't."

Maybe it was his Amish upbringing. She could respect that. She believed it was the right way anyway. Living together sure as heck hadn't worked out for her.

She wanted to ask a bunch of questions. Wanted to figure out where he was coming from and what prompted his offer, but she decided not to look a gift horse in the mouth. She'd given up men, sure. But there was no doubt in her mind this was the right thing for her children. "I'll do it."

THREE DAYS LATER, CORA and her children sat with Abner in Patty's Diner in Sweet Water, North Dakota, eating supper.

They'd driven twelve hundred miles in two days, and the kids were tired. Abner was tired. Cora's eyes had black rings under them, and she seemed to be on autopilot.

He was kinda happy, though, too. Cora had just married him at the courthouse. They'd had to push pretty hard to make it there before five, but he was now a married man. With six kids.

All he had to do at this point was convince his wife not to leave him. Seemed like the hardest job was ahead.

But he'd convinced her to come to North Dakota. If she hadn't agreed to that, he'd been very tempted to go with her to Huntingdon. Live beside her. Whatever it took. If she'd let him without thinking he was worse than a stalker.

He knew he'd pushed too hard when she kissed him, and he had to back off. He didn't have enough time to do things slow, though. And he didn't know what to say. What to do. Did he apologize for that kiss? He wasn't sorry. Not for the kiss. He was just sorry about the way she felt.

Regardless, now he held Luna on his lap, giving her pieces of his cooked carrots and peas and little bites of his chicken. Cora fed Claire in the highchair, and the other kids were in the booth, two beside him and two beside Cora.

The kids were talking, wiggling, but Cora and he were quiet, despite the fact that they'd not talked the whole way here because they'd driven separately. He'd taken his motorcycle to the car dealer and come back with an SUV. Not the way he might normally buy a vehicle, but he'd needed to do something. He'd rather have a family than a bike, and that hadn't been a hardship.

The bell over the door jingled, and a blast of cold air hit their table. Abner put a pea into Luna's mouth and looked up.

"Hey, Abner." Preacher, his harvest crew boss from the past summer, walked in with his wife, Reina.

"Preacher." Abner nodded, not even trying to contain his grin when Preacher walked over, his eyes moving around the table, noting Cora and marking each child. "This is my wife, Cora."

Abner didn't give any extra explanation. He had just finished up with the crew less than three weeks ago, didn't have a girlfriend, and had no plans on getting married.

Preacher barely blinked. "You've multiplied since I saw you last."

Abner's lips twitched. "Can't outwork me, bro."

Preacher smiled. "Didn't know it was work."

Reina elbowed him. "It's work."

Preacher held his hand out to Cora. "Good to meet you, Cora. I'm Clay, since your deadbeat husband was raised in a barn and never learned manners."

Cora gave Clay a pleasant smile while she shook his hand, but Abner noted the lines of fatigue around her face and the droop of her shoulders. He wanted to get her home and let her rest. He shouldn't have pushed for them to travel so hard and fast.

"And I'm Reina. Since my husband was apparently raised in the same barn." Reina held her hand out, and Cora shook it.

Clay put an arm around his wife. "Does this mean we're sleeping in the barn tonight for old time's sake?"

Reina's smile was intimate, and Abner almost looked away. "I think it'd be fun to sleep in the barn."

"Even if I say I'm sleeping with my .22 to shoot rats?"

"I get the gun. You can hold the spotlight."

Abner glanced at Cora. A smile hovered around her lips. He turned back to Preacher. "You two sound like you're going to have a lot of fun tonight, but where's Gina?" he asked, referring to their daughter.

"She's with my mom. Reina and I are leaving pretty early in the morning to go look at a few farms for sale."

"You getting out of the harvesting business?"

Clay nodded. "Mack's gonna buy it," he said, referring to one of the other crew members. "He's at home in Oklahoma now, but he's coming up next week to talk."

They chatted a little longer, then Clay and Reina went to find a seat.

"I'm gonna go pay. You good?"

She gave him a look that said she'd been handling her six kids by herself for a long time and he hadn't needed to ask.

He paused before standing. "Did you want me to leave without asking?"

Her shoulders slumped. "No. I'm sorry. I'm tired and grumpy."

"We're almost home." He couldn't keep his lips from turning up in a huge smile. There was the nagging thought that Cora might not like him enough to stay, but otherwise, he was thrilled to his toenails that he was back in the state he loved with the seven people who meant more to him than anything else in the world.

He pushed aside and, carrying Luna, walked to the cash register, pulling out his wallet.

He knew their waitress, Angela, not that they were on great speaking terms, but enough to be friendly.

"How was your meal, Abner?" she asked.

"Best meal I had all day," he said. She looked a little rougher than she had when he'd seen her in Nebraska, and he never had found out why she'd come to Sweet Water. But he felt a little bad for her. She'd been conniving and done a few things that he'd say were dead wrong, but who hadn't? It was pretty obvious to him that she'd been down a rough road, and it looked like she'd been doing some learning in the school of hard knocks.

"Are you with relatives?" Her tone was polite and friendly, but not suggestive or flirtatious, and he answered easily.

"My wife and kids."

Her hand with his change in it hung suspended over his. Her mouth opened and closed. "Your wife?"

Abner just raised his brow.

"I didn't see you as the marrying kind." She dropped the change in his hand.

It was a fact he'd been grateful for. "I'm not. Only for Cora. You'll have to come out and visit."

Angela's eyes widened. Abner felt bad for her because from her reaction he felt like maybe the townspeople hadn't been real welcoming.

"Give me your number, and I'll give it to my wife. I think she'd love company, and I've seen you at the church; you're good with kids."

"You have a lot of them," Angela said as she grabbed a pen and scribbled her number on the back of her order pad. "Are they all yours?"

"Yes." The word was out of his mouth before he thought about it. He'd never even talked to Cora about their fathers or what his role would be. Maybe that's because she wasn't planning on staying.

"I'm going to have some interesting conversations with your wife." So was he.

Chapter 16

They arrived at Abner's ranch well after dark. There was a moon and a few inches of snow on the ground so it wasn't completely black, but that might have been better.

The house was small. Tiny. Even smaller than the house in Ohio. Cora had no idea where they were all going to stay.

There was a barn. It looked big and black in the night.

No pole lights. No neighbors. Nothing but wind and miles of snow-blanketed flat land in all directions.

"No animals?" she asked Abner when she parked beside him at the side of the house and he walked to her car. What was a ranch without animals? Shouldn't there be a dog and some cattle and a few ducks or goats or something? Isn't that what real ranches had? Maybe everything was sleeping. It was night.

"Can't have animals when I'm not here."

Oh. Of course. Right. She knew that.

Not.

What exactly had made her think coming to the middle of nowhere was a good idea for her children? And for her?

If she had any doubts, any at all, about whether Abner was an ax murderer, she'd be turning around and leaving. She wouldn't even stay the night. She could scream as loud as she wanted to, and no one would hear. Not a soul.

Her younger children were sleepy in the back seat, but Derrick, who'd ridden with her, and Andrew, who'd ridden with Abner, were both out and excited.

He wore a t-shirt and didn't seem cold. She hunkered down in her hooded sweatshirt and wished she'd worn her coat instead of packing it.

Running a hand over his head, he said, "I have one room off the side of the house. That's where the moving company was supposed to put the bunk beds up, and I'll get to work immediately tomorrow adding on."

"You can do that?"

"Yeah. It's not been too cold here, and only the first couple of inches of ground are frozen. I'll be—"

"Wait. What? Couple of inches? Frozen ground? What are you talking about?"

His smile came out slow, and her heart grinned in return.

"Forgot you were a southern girl."

"Ohio is hardly the Deep South."

"Almost Kentucky. West Virginia. Same hills." He shook his head like there was something wrong with her.

"You're from the same place," she said, unable to not smile, despite her tiredness.

He turned serious. "I love what I've done between now and then, but I do have a major regret about leaving. That won't ever change."

She was too tired to think about that tonight. "I meant you can build a room onto your house?"

"Yeah." He looked down. Then, like he'd made a deliberate decision to say more, he said, "That's what my dad did. I worked full-time with him for a couple of years. I can build something that probably won't fall down or leak. Long's the kids do their running and jumping outside."

"You might as well forget it then. Maybe we should just stay in the barn. Is there heat?"

"No." He grunted. "Think I can get a few fellows to come help me. Next week this time, the kids will have two rooms."

"They're not going to have a problem sleeping wherever." And she had the play yard for Claire. Her abs tensed, and she felt a little like throwing up. "Where am I sleeping?"

"There's a loft. I didn't want to worry about the kids falling down the stairs, and it's a lot smaller." A big shoulder lifted. "You can sleep with the kids if you want."

"You?" There were things they'd never talked about, and maybe they should. But this wasn't going to be one of them.

He stared down at her, and she wished the moon were brighter. "Guess that depends on where you want me."

That hardly seemed right. "What do you want?"

He dismissed her almost immediately. "I have a lot of dreams but only a couple of things I feel like I can't live without. Maybe we'll talk about it someday, but we've stood around long enough. I'll sleep in the barn."

He turned back to his vehicle, opened the door, and started unbuckling Luna.

Derrick and Andrew had already been to the house and had the lights on. Cora sent a worried glance that way. "The door wasn't locked," she called over to Abner. "Do you think someone broke in?"

"Never lock it. Not even sure Boone had a key."

"Boone?"

"I bought it from him."

"Oh." She felt like she moved to a different country. They didn't lock their doors? Abner didn't seem worried about the boys, and she knew from the past few weeks that he wouldn't let them get into anything that would hurt them, so she tried not to worry either.

The house wasn't much to look at, which didn't surprise Cora. The kitchen seemed functional, and there was a bathroom with a shower-tub combo.

She didn't bathe the kids, though. Just changed a diaper and put the younger four to bed, staying in the room and singing softly until they drifted off. With a set of bunks along opposite walls and Luna's little daybed pushed against the far wall, there was not much space at all.

Abner had taken the two older boys out to the barn, so she took a quick shower and climbed the stairs to the loft.

She had to use her flashlight app because there was no light. Bare wood floor and a small window. So low she probably couldn't stand upright. Well, she'd go back down and find the blankets they'd packed in the car.

The boys were in, and she kissed them good night before putting her shoes back on.

"Where're you going?" Abner asked from the sink where he'd gotten a drink of water.

"Getting blankets for upstairs. And I'll get tomorrow's clothes while I'm at it." For herself and the kids and there was a list of things a mile long to do.

"Uh..."

She stopped. Abner didn't usually have a problem speaking. So she knew whatever he was going to say was probably more difficult than usual. Putting her shoe down, she gave him her full attention.

He shoved his hands in his pockets. "I know it's kinda late, but I thought maybe you'd like to walk around a bit?"

As she looked at him, light dawned. He cared what she thought. He wanted her to like it. Her opinion mattered to him.

That realization made her next words the truth. "I'd love to."

His smile was worth it. She finished putting her shoes on. When she straightened, he put a coat around her shoulders.

"Rather than dig yours out," he said.

"Thanks." She shoved her arms in and closed her eyes. It smelled like Abner and all the good things from outside.

"Sleeping on your feet?"

She jerked her eyes open. "I guess." Not exactly.

"Too tired?"

"No."

He opened the door, and she stepped through. The air was crisp as it had been before, but she took the time now to lift her face to the sky and breath deep. It felt like her lungs were being cleaned out. Like the wholesome, unpolluted air drove out all the impurities that had been collecting in her body. Fanciful, probably, but that's the way it felt.

"You should have a hat on. Your hair's wet."

"I should cut it." Long hair was a vanity with small children.

"Don't."

"You don't have to mess with it every day."

"I get to look at it. It's pretty." He stepped off the porch and reached back, holding out his hand for her. "I'll fix it. Just tell me what to do. I've done Luna's."

He had. And she loved watching that. There was nothing in the world more appealing to her than a man who was good with kids. Her kids. That's why Abner was so dangerous to her heart.

She placed her hand in his and stepped off the porch. "I'll hold you to that, then."

He didn't let go of her hand, and she didn't pull it away.

They walked in silence to the corral and on to the barn. "There's some holes in the floor, and it's not really the shape to suit our purposes. It was built back when everyone baled small bales. The big bales we do now don't really stack in here well."

"You need to build another barn?"

"No. Not really. It's cheaper to wrap the bales to protect them from the weather. Just chatting, I guess."

"Keep chatting. It doesn't always make sense to me, but I suppose I should learn."

"I guess we're both learning."

She turned to him. Surprised. "I thought you knew about animals and farms and stuff."

He grunted. "There's always more to learn. I guess I meant...other things."

"Like?" she prompted, completely lost.

They'd moved to the other side of the barn where there was a small fenced area. She had no idea what it was called or what it was for.

"Like...it seems like every time I try to tell you how I feel, you get mad at me or turn away."

She opened her mouth, but he put a hand up.

"My fault. I know it's my fault. But that's what I need to learn." He put a foot up on the railing and leaned on it. He spoke slowly, like he was looking for the right thing. "I want to learn how to talk to you, how to..."

She waited, and he sighed, frustrated.

"I thought, at the first bonfire we had, that I was doing pretty good. That you were laughing and seemed to like me. But then everything went bad, and I haven't been able to figure out what I did or how to fix it."

He turned to her. "If you went to Huntingdon, I thought about following you."

She gasped.

"I was. Call me a stalker, call me crazy, I don't know. Maybe it's true. I just know I've been around all over, and there's not a single woman anywhere that fits my heart like you."

"You don't know me. You don't know who I am or what I've done."

"I knew you before any of that."

"I've changed."

"I can see it. You've matured. Even your scent has changed."

"My scent?"

He grinned and hung his head a little. "Yeah. It used to be like cotton candy, but it's a little less sweet now, huskier or something. I don't know. It drives me crazy. I smell it, and I just want to touch you."

She had to laugh over that. "I can't believe that. I've never seen you struggle."

"I'm struggling now."

Her eyes swept over him. "I don't see it."

"Maybe you're not looking."

She closed the distance between them, feeling confident. His words had given her that feeling. The fact that he cared what she thought and wanted to do right by her.

"I'm looking at you pretty close, and I still don't see the struggle."

He took his hands and held them up. Fisted. "I want to touch you. When you walk by. When you stand at the stove and laugh at something Luna said. When you yell at the boys for wrestling. When you bend over to kiss them good night. When you're sweeping the floor. When you change diapers." He closed his mouth like he would say more but felt he'd said enough. "It's a constant struggle."

"Now?"

"Especially now."

She put a tentative hand on his chest and tried to swallow past the tightness in her chest. "Don't struggle."

He hissed out a breath. "I have to. I can't give in because you think that's all I want."

She could see the fight in his eyes. Now. But they were honest and sincere, too.

"I'm not gonna lie," he said softly. "I want that. Of course I do. But that's not all I want."

"What else is there?" She knew, of course, but she wanted to know what he would say.

"I want to know that you feel the same. If you don't, then that there's a chance you will. I want to know what I can do...to make you fall in love with me."

She touched the top rail of the fence, for some reason not wanting him to know how she felt. "I don't think you can make anyone do that."

"Are you saying there's no hope?"

He'd just shared so much. It wasn't right for her to hide. She opened her mouth and pushed the words out before her brain could stop them. "I'm saying I like you a lot. It scares me how much. I've depended on men before, and it's been a bust. I wanted to stand on my own two feet. And yet, here I am, dependent once more."

He stared at her, as though processing what she'd said. Maybe he was trying to think of an argument. But there wasn't one. It was how she felt. He couldn't argue with feelings.

"So," he said slowly. "You like me, but you want to be independent."

"Yes." It was a firm word. Abner wasn't like any of the other men she'd been with, but that didn't change the fact that she needed to be able to support herself and her children.

"Where does that leave us, then?" he asked, and he sounded sad. It hurt her heart and made her feel a nagging thought that maybe she was not making the best decision. But she knew she was. What could be better for her children than a mother who didn't depend on anyone but herself?

"Well, we're here." She hadn't thought any farther than that.

"And we're married."

Yeah. That was a little hard to remember. But she'd done it for Abner, and it could be annulled.

"You wanted to be friends," she stated.

"You were against that."

"Because I didn't like you like a friend."

Silence, like shocked silence, filled the air. Loud, big silence.

"How, exactly, do you like me?"

"I guess it is a little like a friendship, because I like to laugh with you and play with you and work beside you, but..." She took a breath, knowing that what she was going to say almost completely contradicted what she'd said before, and she didn't know how the sides fit together, she just knew she was both. "I also liked kissing you."

"I didn't think you did." His mouth barely moved, like she'd shocked him again.

"What made you think that?" She tried to remember what had happened to make him think that, but she couldn't.

"I don't know. You walked away. You didn't talk to me. You seemed to avoid me." He lifted a finger and ran it down her cheek. "I liked it so much, I guess I didn't even have a clue what you were thinking."

"Let me help you." She took a breath, her logical thought telling her she was foolish to give away more than she had but her heart longing for him to know. "It was the best kiss I've ever had."

"Me too," he said simply, his hand lightly touching her cheek before sliding around and cupping it. "I've never wanted to kiss anyone else."

She pressed her cheek into his hand, but her eyes popped open at his statement. "Have you?"

"I guess if we're going to talk about my past, we should talk about yours, too."

Her face fell, and she pulled back some.

"Don't. Please." His hand stilled. "I'm not holding anything against you, as I hope you don't me, and it doesn't matter. Won't change a thing. But tonight, the waitress asked me if they were all my kids, and I didn't even think about it. I said yes." He ran his thumb over her cheekbone. "Are there going to be men who want to visit their children? Are we going to have to let them go? Who are these guys? I don't even know. When she asked me that, I felt like I didn't even know my family. And I want to. Even the bad and ugly parts."

She stepped closer and put her arms around his waist, needed that comfort. He didn't disappoint, of course, and wrapped her in his arms, pulling her to him and tucking her head under his chin. "It feels like you belong right here. Nothing has ever felt more right to me."

"No other girls?" She pinched her mouth closed.

"What if I don't want to admit what I have or haven't done?"

"Me either."

"That probably means we should."

"Yeah, I know."

"Let's do that some other time."

"That's a great idea."

"I don't know what we're going to do about the other, though."

She sighed, snuggling closer. "Yeah. I don't know either."

"Can we think about that?"

"Yeah. We'll talk about that later, too."

Chapter 17

The next day was busy as they unpacked the cars and Cora took care of all the kids' clothes and things.

He helped her some, more by carrying Luna around with him and having the boys out from underfoot. He measured and did some figuring, then ordered lumber, hardware, and metal, and made some phone calls.

Sometimes it was annoying how fast gossip traveled in a small town, but at other times, like this, it was helpful. He'd have a few guys here tomorrow when the lumber came, enough to help him dig holes and set the footers in ready-mix cement, then the next day, there'd be an army and he'd have it under roof.

He had one more phone call to make, but he was saving it for lunchtime when he knew Jeb would be in.

Cora had smiled at him today. He thought maybe their talk last night had cleared the air between them some. He'd admitted to some things that had been hard, but he couldn't expect to reap benefits without taking a risk. True in business and true in life and relationship. Not that he was any expert on relationships. Far from it.

But he did think that he'd made some progress with Cora.

So, it kind of took him by surprise when he left the boys outside picking up rocks and came in to make his call. Cora was in the bedroom putting the kids down, and he didn't really mean to eavesdrop, but he thought he heard his name, which made him smile. Maybe the kids would always call him Abner. Maybe eventually he'd be "Dad."

He moved toward the door, thinking he'd go in and see them before their nap, since they were obviously asking about him, but he stopped at the door.

"I don't know how long we're going to stay with him, honey. Mommy's going to get a job, and we're going to move out as soon as we can."

Maybe she said something else, but he couldn't hear because of the blood rushing in his ears. It felt like his ribs cracked, too, but maybe that was just his heart breaking.

THE BOYS WERE REALLY upset with Cora when she insisted that they had to go get registered at the school rather than watch the men dig the holes and put the footers in. Abner had watched her with a hooded gaze as she'd made the announcement then watched some more as the boys had used their best arguments, and some that weren't so good, to get out of it.

In the end, she'd won, of course, and this morning, the bus had picked them up along with Summer and Kohlton who was registered for three-year-old preschool.

The house felt empty and sad without them. She could have gone out and watched the men herself, but she'd have had to keep the little ones out of the way, and she didn't want to risk them getting hurt.

So she called the waitress that Abner had gotten the number for, Angela. She had the morning off and offered to come right out.

"We'll cook lunch for the men. Tell Abner we'll have it ready at noon."

"There must be at least twenty men out there."

"We've got it."

Maybe *she* had it.

Cora could cook, but for twenty men? Wasn't happening. She'd gone to the grocery store when she'd registered the kids, but she hadn't gotten anything that would feed twenty. She almost wished she hadn't called her.

Claire was down for her morning nap and Cora had Luna on her hip when she answered the door.

"My goodness, it's cold out there." Angela blew in like a tornado, carrying a ten-pound bag of hamburger and a larger bag of potatoes, plus another bag of assorted groceries. "It's not going to take us long to make this, but we'd better not mess around. Men get cranky when they're hungry."

She grunted a laugh, and her blue eyes sparkled. Her blond-white hair made her look like an angel, and her slim build, evident under her green sweater and khaki skirt, made Cora conscious of her own curves.

"I'm Angela, by the way." There was a certain reserve in her movements, but her energy was infectious and her confidence unmatched.

Cora shook her hand. "Cora."

"And you've been married to Abner for how long?" she asked as she set the food on the table. "We need to pare the potatoes and cook the meat. Do you have a pan big enough?"

Cora had no idea.

They ended up using four—two for the potatoes and two for the meat.

"Do you want to pare or cook?" Angela talked a lot, but it wasn't a fast talking. Cultured. "And I did bring some broccoli, and we can cook it with cheese, but none of those guys are going to eat any. I have a few pies in my car. Apple, of course. Can't carry everything at once. We'll get those later. They're made, but they need to be baked."

Cora's head spun. She ended up with a wooden spoon in her hand, standing at the stove with Luna on one hip, stirring the meat as it browned.

"So you never did answer me. How long have you and Abner been married?"

"Not long," Cora hedged. She was pretty sure this was the person that Abner had told all the children were his. "You seem pretty confident in the kitchen."

"My dad's a pastor. I grew up working in church dinners. Christmas, Thanksgiving, Bible school, Sunday lunches, men's prayer breakfasts, ladies' meetings, you name it, I worked in the kitchen and washed every last dang dish. Excuse the Baptist swearing, but growing up, I had to be perfect, seen but not heard, discreet, chaste, and with the proper reserve. Now, I'm out of the house, and I can say dang if I want to. There's no rule in the Bible against it."

"I suppose not."

"It took me a while to figure out that I could be me and not the puppet my dad always wanted me to be."

"I see."

"So, about you and Abner."

"Yes, we're married."

Angela waved a potato in one hand, which wasn't bad, and her knife in the other, which was slightly scary. "How long, girlfriend?"

Cora stared at the stove, focused on the meat. "Three days."

"No, *crap*." She drew that word out, then... "Excuse the Baptist swearing."

"Sure."

"Abner's had a woman on the side all this time? That's crazy. I would *never* have guessed it. He never even looked at a girl, and no wonder, now that I've seen you, but come on. I thought he was one of those...what are they called when there's no attraction to male or female?" She waved her knife in the air again. It really made Cora want to duck.

"Asexual?"

"Yes!" She pointed the knife in the air like a sword. "That's it." She went back to paring potatoes. "I mean he just seemed so...uninterested." She laughed. "Six kids. Guess he was interested all right."

"Well," Cora began. She couldn't let her continue to think a lie. That's what had gotten her in trouble in the first place all those years ago. "They're not his."

"What? He said they were."

"Well, he is the only one that acts like a dad. But no."

"He always was good with the kids at church. They followed him around like the Pied Piper."

"Yeah, he's great with them."

"Well, it's a good thing he married you. Now you've got it made in the shade."

Cora figured that's exactly what people would think, but she was happy it didn't merit a knife shake. "I actually got an email this morning about a job in Cincinnati. I might be taking the kids and leaving."

Angela stopped paring.

Cora eyed the knife as Angela slowly straightened.

"What?" she said incredulously. Her knife hand was steady as a rock.

"Well, we agreed that this was only temporary, since I don't want to have to depend on a man to take care of me for the rest of my life. I'm bigger and stronger than that. And I'm making decisions now that are best for my children, as much as I can."

"Oh, really?"

"Yes," Cora said firmly. "It sounds like our lives have been completely opposite up to this point, but I'm done needing a man-flavor of the month. I can do this, and I don't need a man to make me feel worthy or be a status symbol."

Angela's perfect face wrinkled. "You're serious."

"Of course. I've made a lot of mistakes, but it's time I steer the direction of my life by myself and not depend on someone else to do it for me."

"I'm sorry, girlfriend, but that's about the dumbest thing I've ever heard."

Cora twisted just a little so her body was between Angela's knife and Luna who was still perched on her hip, slowly and somewhat painfully taking the hair out of Cora's messy bun. "Why?"

"Because you've got a good man who loves you, loves your kids, and you'd walk away from him because of some crap, excuse the Baptist swearing, about being independent? Be independent while you're living here."

"I can't. Everyone is going to say exactly what you just did about me having it made in the shade and how I trapped Abner and how I can't stand on my own."

"You weren't made to stand on your own."

Cora stopped with her mouth open. "Huh?"

"I mean, yeah, some people never get married, and that's fine. But God made man, and he made woman to be a helper fit for him. Marriage is God's way of saying teamwork makes the dream work." Her knife flew around the potato she held in her hand. "I mean, the best basketball player in the world doesn't go out on the floor by himself and say he can't have teammates because he's got to prove to himself and the rest of the world that he can win on his own, right?"

"Yeah, but that's basketball. A sprinter does it on her own."

"Life isn't a sprint, and marriage isn't a game. With a few exceptions, God meant for adults to team up. Two by two."

"That's the ark."

"I'm a pastor's daughter. I can tell you about the ark backward, upside down, inside out, and in Hebrew." She smirked and grabbed another potato.

"But that's not the way the world works now."

"It's the world that changed. Not God."

"You've got to change with the times."

"He made you. Don't you think he knows what you need and how you work? Society changes, but nothing ever changes with God. Now *that's* in the Bible, dang it." She punched the air with her knife and opened her mouth, but Cora beat her to it.

"Excused."

They grinned.

Dinner was a success, and when Angela left, Cora considered her a friend, even if they disagreed. Abner took the boys and went out to work some on the room, which was all under roof.

After they put the kids to bed, Abner grabbed her hand and pulled her out of their room. "Come out and look at it. I think you'll be impressed."

She had to smile at his enthusiasm. "I'm ready for you to impress me."

"Not me. The room, silly." But his hand squeezed hers, and his mood was lighthearted and happy as he showed her the work that had been accomplished lit by several work lights scattered around the room. The windows were framed and just needed to be put in. A stack of drywall sat on the floor, and wires ran through the exposed studs to where light sockets and switches would be and also to a light on the ceiling.

"So, what do you think?" Abner's eyes glowed, and she hadn't seen him this animated about anything.

"I think it's great." She meant it. No one had ever built her children a room before.

"I don't know if we should put the boys in this room or give the bigger room to the girls. And it only has to last until next year, hopefully, because I fully intended when I bought the place to build a house. We just can't live so cramped up through the winter and next summer. And the materials weren't that bad." He put both hands on his head and looked around the room. "I'm sorry. I've been talking so much, you haven't had a chance to say anything."

He looked at her and must have been able to tell that she was more worried about telling him about her interview than being interested in the room. The glow left his face, and his brows drew in.

Maybe it was easier to focus on trying to get a job than it was to think that someone spent this kind of money and work and time on her and her children.

Angela had said it was because he loved her. Maybe he did. Maybe she loved him, too. But that shouldn't change anything. Should it?

"Hey, what's wrong?" he asked, coming toward her.

She looked at the particleboard floor, taking a steadying breath. "I got an email today from one of the places where I'd put an application in online."

"Oh?"

"They want to interview me."

"That's great."

She peeked up at him, and he truly looked happy for her.

"Is it going to be like a video call or something? This is for online work?"

"The interview is in Cincinnati."

His smile tightened, and he looked to the window, out into the blackness beyond. "When?" He didn't look at her.

"Monday."

"So you'll need to fly out Sunday morning."

"I figured I'd drive. It'll be cheaper."

"We just drove that. It takes two days, and it's exhausting."

"I'll take the little ones with me, but I was really hoping I could ask you—"

"You can leave them all here. I'll drive you to the airport on Sunday, and I'll pick you up on Tuesday. We can buy your ticket right now."

"You don't have to do that."

"I want to." It looked like he wanted to say more, but he didn't, pulling his phone out of his pocket and punching into it.

"Come on," he said. "It's cold out here. The heat still needs to be hooked up, too."

He turned the lights out, and they walked out. Cora's heart beat sickly in her chest. She should be happy. She was going for an interview. If she got the job, it would be the best one she ever had. But she'd be moving her children yet again, and a thousand miles away from Abner.

They went into the kitchen, and she cut him a slice of the leftover apple pie while he got her information and bought her a plane ticket. It wasn't really standing on her own two feet if Abner helped her every step of the way, but if she got the job, she'd only need a few months until she was able to do it on her own.

"It's cold out, but we could take a walk."

She remembered her promise to tell him about the kids' fathers. She wanted to fulfill it in case she really did get the job and really did leave. He deserved that much.

Plus, she was curious about him.

Chapter 18

It was selfish to hope she didn't get the job. Abner knew that. He couldn't bring himself to hope that she did, but he could keep from praying that she didn't.

If that was what she wanted and it made her happy, he needed to step out of the way and let her go.

Head knowledge.

But his heart rebelled. He wanted to convince her to stay. If she didn't, he wanted to go with her.

He wanted to, but he knew he wouldn't, because that's not where he belonged.

He held the door while she walked through, the cold air funneling in. The wind North Dakota was known for. She hunkered down in her jacket. He lifted his face to the wind.

Cold, hot, it didn't matter when one was on the roof, he kept working. Couldn't stop because his hands were cold or he couldn't feel his feet or he thought he'd pass out from the heat or, more likely, die of thirst. Better get all the nails pounded in before he inconvenienced everyone by kicking the bucket.

It wasn't pleasant then, but it had taught him self-denial and character. Now, the feel of the wind across the flatland, especially in the dark and cold, it touched something wild in his soul, and he couldn't help but lift his head, almost like answering a challenge.

Yeah, he'd found the land he was born to love. He wasn't leaving it.

He slid his hand into Cora's as they walked off the steps and tucked their joined hands in his pocket. He didn't want her fingers to get cold.

They walked out the drive, past the barn, and continued on. The silence between them felt right and natural.

"Wow," Cora said. "It's so...amazing out here." She huffed out a breath. "It didn't feel friendly the night we arrived. Maybe it's because you're beside me, but the land feels alive, almost. Like it has a spirit."

"Maybe there's less stuff to distract you and it's easier to feel God." That's kind of how he felt.

"Jason is Andrew's father, and we're the only two who know it."

He stopped walking. She didn't turn to face him but lifted her head to the sky.

"Stephen is Derrick and Summer's father. We lived together for a while. Got married. He cheated. I left and came back a few times. It was a mess. A lot of fighting and I started going to bars. He finally ran off with someone else, and I was a disaster. A lot of drinking, a lot of different men, and I don't know who Kohlton's father is. I don't even know if I spent more than one night with him."

He squeezed her hand, which was limp in his pocket. "You don't have to tell me this."

"You're right. You should know. People ask, and it's kind of weird that you don't know the fathers of your wife's children." She snorted without humor. "It's sad that your wife doesn't know the father of your wife's children."

"I wish I could go back and do that one thing differently."

"I lived with another guy; he was from New Jersey. And yes, I know how babies are made, and yes, I know about the newfangled invention of birth control, but I had four small children and was working nights at the all-night diner, studying graphic design when it was slow, and taking care of the kids during the day while he worked. Time slipped by, and I forgot. He left when Luna wasn't quite two months, and neither of us knew I was pregnant with Claire. I was, however, awarded child support for two children. I get it once in a while, when he decides to work." She lifted her hand up then let it down, slapping her leg. "There. That's the whole sordid story of my life."

She turned to him. "You see now what the issue is?" She tugged at her hand, but he wouldn't let it go. "I kept thinking all I needed was a man who would stay. A good man. And it was a lie. I needed to buck up and do it myself." The wind blew her sigh away. "Angela said that God meant for a man and a woman to team up. And that might be true. But I've gone so far from what God intended that there's no hope for me."

Abner's heart felt like a piece of wood, hard in his chest. But he opened his mouth, because he still had hope. "I was thinking about the woman at the well."

Cora's head turned.

"You know," he continued. "She had five husbands, and the man she was living with when she met Jesus wasn't her husband."

"Yeah, I know the story," Cora said.

"It's a story that's been read by millions of people. Her life is immortalized forever because God's word shall never pass away."

Cora wouldn't look at him, but he kept going. "If her life had been perfect, then she wouldn't have been the perfect woman for that story."

"I guess I don't understand your point."

"You're the perfect woman for my story."

And then she did turn to him. "What is your story, Abner?"

"I waited for you."

She shook her head. "I told you everything."

"So did I."

"Are you serious?"

"As a heart attack." There wasn't a hint of humor in his tone. Because there was nothing to laugh at.

"Then that means..." Her voice trailed off, and her head tilted.

He could only assume that she was thinking about their kiss.

"Yeah."

"Crap." She spun and started walking fast back to the house.

"Cora," he called.

His voice acted like a whip, and she started to run. Just like she had the last time when he'd pushed too hard.

He didn't want to run after her, but he strode toward the house. Could they fix this?

His phone buzzed in his pocket, and he pulled it out. Luke. He'd been back in New Zealand for several weeks. Abner swiped the bar and answered.

"Yeah?"

"Hey, man, what's up?"

He thought about saying he'd gotten married, but he really didn't want to get into the whole complicated situation.

"Not much." What a lie.

"Well, hey, I'm slammed, but I got a gig planting cotton in Australia. Too much for me to handle solo. It's gonna be through the holiday season. Don't matter to me, and figured since you don't have no family, wouldn't matter to you, either."

At this point, Abner would typically say "when can you pick me up from the airport," but he couldn't. He wouldn't go if Cora were staying. If she left...

"How soon do you need to know?"

Two beats of surprised silence.

"I should start next week. Moving the equipment over the weekend." His breath huffed over the phone. "I really can't wait."

"Then don't. I can't give you an answer right now. You keep looking. I'll call you and see where you're at when I know for sure I can do it."

"Something wrong?"

That was about as close as any of the guys on the crew would get to prying.

"Personal stuff."

Another silence. Abner would bet that Luke was trying to figure out what a single man with no family could be dealing with that fell under the heading "personal stuff," but that's all he was gonna say.

"I'll talk to you next week," Abner said.

"Sure. Take it easy. And hey..."

"Yeah?"

"Call me if you need me. I'm on the other side of the world, but you know I'll come."

"I know. Thanks."

He swiped the phone and hung up, unsure if that was God's timing or just a distraction, but knowing if Cora left, he'd be in Australia over Christmas.

CORA WALKED THROUGH the small airport, pulling her luggage behind her. She'd aced the interview. Funny how when she stopped caring how she did, her nervousness disappeared and she did better than she dreamed she could.

But she didn't care. Alone in the hotel room on Sunday night, sitting in the absolute silence by herself, with only her own thoughts to pick at her, she'd had time to do a lot of thinking.

She missed her kids. Missed the happy chaos. She couldn't say she missed the inevitable fighting, but she missed the feeling of family and the security of home.

She hadn't felt the security of home until Abner had walked into Aunt Sandy's house. None of the other men she'd ever been with had changed the atmosphere of the house and made it homey.

There was a physical attraction. Scarier than anything she'd felt with anyone else. But that's when it hit her, lying on her bed in her hotel room.

She hadn't wanted to depend on anyone, most of all, a man. She'd done it for too long, and that was true.

But what Angela said had come to her mind, and for the first time, Cora realized that two people making a team wasn't just her needing Abner.

It was Abner needing her.

Him standing in the room he was building, almost bubbling over with excitement, wanting to show her what he was doing. His desire to have her with him and walk her around the farm and point out everything. The love and laughter that filled his home.

The fact that he'd waited just for her.

He needed her to fill the empty areas in his life, just as much as she needed him. A symbiotic relationship. Of course.

Once she figured that out, she didn't care about the interview anymore, because she knew she wasn't taking the job.

Of course, that's when the call from Bob had come.

She hadn't spoken with him for long, but he'd just happened to be going west this coming week to visit his relatives in Montana for an early Christmas celebration, since he couldn't get off over Christmas, and promised to stop in.

She hadn't believed him. And she didn't care anyway. She wasn't sure how things stood between Abner and her—they'd not really talked since she'd run from him—but everything that she was going to decide hinged on what he was doing and how he felt.

The couple that was walking in front of her turned off toward the car rental desk, and Abner stood just thirty feet away, framed by the huge windows and the North Dakota sky and prairie, Claire in his arms and Luna holding tight to his hand. Kohlton and Summer pressed close against him, and Andrew looked up at him, earnestly talking while Derrick listened.

He wore jeans and boots and a red button-down, and he looked tall and rugged with the beard he'd never shaved and the cowboy hat that shaded the upper half of his face.

Abner shook his head and laughed. Andrew and Derrick cracked up with him.

But almost like he could feel her gaze, his head lifted and his eyes landed on her. His laughter faded, leaving a small smile hovering around lips that tightened just a little as insecurity lightly brushed over his face.

Her breath caught, and it hit her how ridiculously stupid and self-ish she'd been. Not wanting to depend on a man, thinking it necessary for her personal growth, but never thinking that the man wanted, maybe needed, her to depend on him. As he depended on her.

That what they could have together was so much more beautiful than what they could have apart.

She couldn't stop her mouth from smiling, and his widened grin answered hers.

Her boys saw her and came running, Summer and Kohlton trailing behind, and even Luna pulled on Abner's hand, trying to pull him toward her mother.

Abner stood back, still holding Claire, as Cora bent and hugged her kids.

As happy as she was to see them—she wasn't used to being separated from them for days—she didn't take as much time as she normally might have, because she was happy to see someone else, too.

She straightened, the kids' chattering precluding anything she might have said, but able at least to look into his eyes.

He tilted his head and lifted a brow, as though asking how it had gone.

Maybe she was being bold, but she walked quickly forward, giving him an answering smile before stepping into his arms and hugging both him and Claire. He was solid and warm and breathed in the scent she loved.

It took about two seconds before his arm came around her and he pulled her closer. It felt like coming home, beautiful and complete. She had so much she wanted to say and more that she really needed to, but this wasn't the place.

"I missed you," she whispered instead as she lifted her head and looked up, keeping her arms tight around him.

Claire patted her cheek, but seemed perfectly happy to stay in his arm, and her children chattered around them, but it felt like they were the only two in the world as he looked down, his eyes glowing.

"I missed you more."

She laughed on a puff of breath. "We can fight about that."

His mouth curved up, slow. "Later."

Claire finally reached out her hands, and Cora took the baby, stepping back, her fingers brushing Abner's, and the crazy pings that zinged up her arms and down her ribcage had multiplied since she'd been gone. Or maybe since she'd realized she wanted to stay and nothing else mattered.

Claire's arms tightened around her neck, and Cora hugged her precious baby close. She wouldn't have left her six children with any other man she'd ever been with, and certainly none of those men would have met her at the airport calmly, with her six kids and a smile.

She breathed in the scent of North Dakota-covered baby mixed with the deeper, rugged scent of Abner.

Abner leaned closer and spoke in her ear. "You have anything you want to do in town?"

She leaned her head up, her cheek brushing his. "No. I just want to go home."

His eyes flashed, surprise then maybe triumph. "We have a surprise for you."

"Don't tell her!" Derrick said, in a voice that was not allowed inside.

"I tell Mommy," Kohlton said.

"I tell," Luna repeated.

"Let's not tell her. Let's show her. Okay, guys?" Abner's eyes beamed like they had when he'd shown her the room he was building, spreading warmth and contentment through her veins. She had to smile back. He made it seem like life wasn't so hard. Like it was fun and meant to be enjoyed. With six kids, that was a pretty big accomplishment, but she had to admit it was easier with two adults. When it was just her, it was all she could do to get the basics done.

The kids babbled and talked as they walked out of the airport and into the chill afternoon air. Abner had Luna in his arms and held Kohlton's hand. Cora carried Claire and held Summer's. The boys walked between them.

They garnered more than a few glances from people walking by. It wasn't a normal sight to see that many children. But Abner didn't seem to care. In fact, he seemed happy. Like spending a few days with a bunch of little kids wasn't the work she knew it to be.

"And Abner is going to buy cows," Derrick was saying.

"Black ones. Because even though they taste the same as red ones, people pay more money for black cows." A month ago, Andrew didn't know anything about cows.

Cora's lips couldn't help but curve up at his tone. Like he really knew what he was talking about. Her eyes shifted to Abner, who was watching her with a guilty grin.

"And chickens," Summer said. "Mr. Abner said we'd get baby chicks. And I get to name them all."

"He said maybe we'd get a goat, but they're awful hard to keep in," Derrick said.

"Oh?" Cora raised her brows.

"Yeah. And maybe this fall, we'll get a couple of pigs and fatten them ourselves, then we can butcher them so we have meat to eat all winter." Andrew looked earnestly at her.

"That sounds like a lot of work." She pursed her lips and gave Abner a look.

"Hey, we needed to talk about something at the supper table, and you weren't here to modulate the discussion. It gets worse."

"Really?"

"We're getting a puppy!" Summer shouted.

"And two kitties." Kohlton skipped and wagged their joined hands.

"This is worse," Cora said. "They're not staying in the house." It might not be her house, but she felt she needed to be firm from the beginning.

"Um..." Abner started. "The boys get to sleep with the cats in their room, and the girls get to have the puppy in theirs."

"Obviously, I cannot leave you alone with my children," Cora said in her haughtiest tone but ruined it by smiling.

"I agree. You definitely need to be here to supervise things." Abner winked at her.

They got the kids in the car and started the long ride back to the ranch. Cora looked around at the landscape with new eyes, because, for the first time, she thought this might be where her roots finally sank deep. She needed to talk to Abner, but she knew how he felt. She just needed to make sure that he knew her heart.

The kids settled down after they'd been driving for a while. Abner looked over at her. "I thought, from the look on your face, that things went well."

"They did," she said honestly. "Much better than I thought they would."

He nodded, looked back at the road.

"I'm hot," a little voice called from the back.

Cora reached up and adjusted the heat for the rear. She was pulling her hand back when Abner's fingers touched her wrist. Light and soft. Her eyes sprang to his. He grinned, his fingers slipping around and entwining with hers.

"I'm sorry about the animals. But the kids were sad and missing you. It was the first thing I thought of to talk about to distract them from their mom being gone. I really was just thinking aloud about the cows, and it kind of snowballed."

She shook her head.

His fingers flexed. "I know you might not be staying, and I just didn't want you to think I was trying to make the kids think there were sides or that I was going behind your back about anything."

"I didn't think that and wouldn't. I don't deserve how kind you've been to me, and I certainly never expected or deserved how you've stepped in with the kids. Thank you for keeping them."

"I've always wanted a big family. Always. From the time I was little and even more so when my Amish mother kicked me out." His shoulder lifted. "It's work, of course. But it's fun, and I love it. Thanks for trusting me with them. Even if they do think we're going to have a zoo now."

"I'm not sure I want to butcher a pig." She wasn't much into blood and death, and it kind of turned her stomach to think of it.

"We did it on the farm growing up twice a year. Our neighbor to the east, Jeb, he's got a dairy farm, and I've been paying him to help with the trim work. He said he'd do one with us. It's a lot of work, but it's fun when the neighbors get together and make it a party."

"Many hands make light work?" Cora couldn't help but ask.

"Yeah." Abner slanted a look, his face seeming a little unsure, like he was trying to dissect her reaction.

"Are we there yet?" a voice called from the back seat.

"Nope," Abner said, his lips curved.

"How much longer?" Derrick called.

Cora grunted a laugh. "A very long time."

"How long?"

"If we're not there by the time you're old enough to get your driver's license, we'll talk."

Chapter 19

Jeb, their neighbor the dairy farmer, was carrying his toolbox out when they pulled in.

Abner reluctantly let go of Cora's hand. "He's gotta get home and milk the cows. He does a fantastic job, but he probably won't talk to you. I've never met a man who said less."

Cora nodded.

Abner had really just been making conversation. He loved talking to her. Seeing the animation on her face, seeing her smile, getting that lifted-brow look that jokingly said he was in trouble.

Sure enough, Abner, carrying Luna and holding Summer's hand, passed Jeb on the walk.

"Thanks, man," he said.

Jeb nodded, the hard angles of his face softening a little at the baby in Abner's arms. Jeb jerked his chin at Cora then walked to his old, beat-up pickup. He was gone shortly after in a rumble of sound and a cloud of smoke.

Andrew stood at the door, his body blocking it. "You can't go in, Mom. Not until we're all in so we can see you."

"It's that big?" She lifted her brows at Abner. "If you got the kids a pet snake, I'm not sure we can still be friends."

"I'm not sure I could blame you about that one," Abner said easily. "No snake?"

"I don't know if I would consider that a good surprise." Abner kept the confident grin on his face, but his stomach was squeezing his backbone. He knew she wouldn't be upset, but he didn't know if she'd love it like he hoped she would.

Of course, he had another surprise that not even the kids knew about. Abner knew she'd love it, but he also knew it would help make up her mind to stay with him, and he kind of wanted her to stay because of him and not because of anything else. Maybe that was dumb on his part.

"Fine, then. Open the door and take the kids in." Cora turned to Abner. "Do you want to go in first, too?"

"Nah. Give me Claire, and I'll follow you in."

She handed the baby to him. "I can't imagine what in the world you guys have done in the three days I was gone."

He didn't answer but leaned down and took Claire in his free hand, breathing deep. "I missed you," he said softly, unable to keep from telling her.

He smiled when she shivered. He hoped she missed him too.

But, no.

"I want to talk to you." Her voice was as low as his, like she didn't want the kids to hear.

"Hey, Mom! We're ready!"

Pulling in a deep breath and throwing a smile on her face, she turned from him and stepped to the door, walking through.

He watched her go, his heart beating with hollow thuds in his chest. Somehow, he didn't figure what she had to say was good. But he'd come to some conclusions while she was gone, and he knew they were right. Just depended now on what she decided.

Following her in, he closed the door and waited. The kids were all bunched on the far side of the kitchen. The door to the old bedroom was open, and the door to the new addition was hung and open as well.

Cora's head moved around the kitchen. It looked pretty much the same as it had when she left. Andrew and Derrick had done the dishes before they'd left to pick her up at the airport, but they'd not put the pans away.

Cora seemed to realize that her surprise wasn't in the kitchen.

She walked slowly to the new addition. "It's finished."

Not quite. Jeb probably hadn't gotten all the trim work done, but they'd been cutting the boards out behind the house to keep the mess out so they could set up the beds.

"Three beds," Cora said. "This must be the girls' room."

"Yep," Andrew said. "Except for one girl."

She twisted and looked at him. "Oh?"

He just grinned.

"Look at the other room, Mommy."

She walked to the old bedroom slowly and stood in the doorway. "It's all for you," Summer blurted out, like she couldn't keep the secret anymore.

"Me? This is my room?"

"Yep. Mr. Abner said that you didn't even have a bed at Aunt Sandy's house, so we went and got you one." Derrick hopped a little on his toes.

"That was fun. We got to lie on the beds and try them out." Andrew might be mature for his age, but he'd had just as much fun as the other kids trying out the mattresses.

Cora put her fingers to her chin and tapped it. Abner's chest started to constrict. She didn't look happy.

"Where are Derrick and Andrew going to sleep?" she asked over her shoulder.

"We get the loft!" Andrew almost shouted.

"Mr. Jeb helped take our beds apart and carry them up the stairs, and Mr. Abner wired up some lights for us. He said it would only be a year until we had a new house, but I want to stay there forever. It's almost like a tree house."

Cora's breath huffed. "You probably won't get any tree houses here. If there's a tree on the ranch, I have yet to see it."

The kids all started talking then, telling her how it happened and how they helped and who was there. Luna wanted down, and Abner set her on the floor.

The boys showed her the loft, and it was a good ten minutes before they got tired of talking and ran off wrestling and playing.

That's when Cora turned to him. "What about you? The kids acted like this was just my room."

"It is." He thought it was something nice that he could do for her, but he'd gotten the impression in the last ten minutes that she was just putting on a happy face for her kids.

"Thanks," she said, looking like she wanted to say more, but a crash and crying kept her from following through.

THE NEXT MORNING AT breakfast, Cora cooked bacon, made toast, and made sure the kids were getting ready for school while Abner made eggs and took care of the little ones. They managed to eat breakfast and get the kids on the bus, leaving them with only Luna and Claire.

Cora had gotten a text just before they sat down to breakfast, and she wasn't sure how to approach Abner about it. Her eggs balled in her stomach, and even her bacon didn't taste that great as she fidgeted with the end of her ponytail and wondered how he was going to take this.

It also bothered her that, in the hubbub of putting the kids to bed the night before, he'd slipped out and she realized he truly meant for the room to be all hers.

She had to assume he slept in the barn.

He'd said she and the children could live with him, and he'd said he wanted more, but she'd declined. Maybe his offer wasn't open anymore, or maybe his feelings had changed. She didn't know why else he'd be making a bedroom just for her.

They really needed to talk. But first...

"Remember I told you about Bob Price?" She was standing at the sink with her hands in the dishwater. He was across the kitchen on his knees, doing something in the wall that had to do with the ductwork and sealing things up after running heat to the new room.

Something clanged, and then it was quiet, except for Claire pounding a wooden spoon on the floor.

"Yeah?" he said.

She couldn't read a thing in his tone.

"He texted me this morning, and he's stopping in on the way to Montana." She said it fast, like he wouldn't be able to ask questions if she spit it out quickly.

And he didn't ask anything.

She supposed she should feel relief, but it only hardened the knot of wire in her stomach.

A few more bangs and clanks and there was movement behind her.

"I'm going outside for a bit."

"Abner? Wait."

He stopped with his hand on the doorknob, facing the door, his tool belt slung over his shoulder.

"I told you that I emailed him."

"I know."

"When I was in Cincinnati, he called me back. He said he was going out to Montana to visit relatives and that he'd stop in, but I really didn't think he would."

When he'd texted, she texted him back saying that today wasn't a great day, but there hadn't been a response.

He turned his head slowly and looked over his shoulder. "Did you tell him you were married?"

She hadn't. "I wasn't sure how things were going to go down with us. When we did it, we said it was just so that you have vows and rings." She laughed, a nervous sound. "We never did get the rings."

"I did."

She must have looked as confused as she felt.

"When we went to get the bed and mattress, I got rings, too. Didn't want to get them without you, but..."

The sound of a pickup interrupted him. He leaned over and glanced out the window. "Jeb's here."

"I'll make sure you guys have lunch."

"Maybe we ought to plan on talking after the kids go to bed. We need to get us straightened out." He looked back toward the door. "I'm not thrilled about Bob being here."

"I didn't think you would be." She actually thought he might be angry about it, but he didn't seem to be. Why did she always have such a hard time telling people no? She should have just told Bob to forget about stopping. She wished she had. Just because it was more important to her to show Abner she cared about him than to appease Bob.

Abner went out, closing the door behind him.

Lunch was over and she had the dishes done and the children in bed when another phone call came. She recognized the Cincinnati area code and answered with trembling fingers.

It was a short call. Less than five minutes and she wondered if she were making a big mistake. It didn't feel like it, but she had never been able to trust her feelings. Not the surface ones anyway.

Bob didn't show up all day, and Cora was starting to think he wasn't going to. Maybe he'd gotten her text and just never responded. That was fine by her.

After supper, she helped the kids with their schoolwork while Abner washed dishes with Summer on a chair and Luna sitting on the counter.

It was dark, of course, and the wind howled outside. She felt a little isolated, but in a cozy, her family was all together way. It was an odd feeling, but one she liked. Only the next time, she was going to sit at the other end of the table so she could look up and stare at Abner all she wanted.

She'd just finished giving Andrew his spelling words and was about to send the older boys to get showered when, above the wind, there was a knock at the door.

She lifted her head and turned to look at Abner, who was already looking at her. His brow lifted in question.

"I don't know," she said in response, assuming that he was asking her if it was Bob.

He didn't say anything but grabbed Luna off the counter and went to the door.

A blast of icy air swept through the room as Abner opened the door and Bob walked in.

Cora's body stiffened like the frozen ground outside.

"Hey, Uncle Bob!" Andrew jumped up and ran over to him.

As he usually did, Bob reached into his shirt pocket and pulled out a candy bar. "Hey, kid. Long time no see."

It was the candy bar that did it. All her other kids, the five that could walk, anyway, went running to Bob.

Abner looked at her, his expression saying, "Are you really going to let the kids eat candy *now?*"

She pushed back and stood, thinking she would walk to him and make sure he understood that she'd texted Bob about not coming after all.

His eyes widened as she walked to him, like he was surprised. Maybe he expected her to be all over welcoming Bob.

But the surprise turned to wariness. And when she reached out to put her arm around him, pressing her body to his and lifting her head, he was as stiff as a statue. His brows had lowered, and his eyes narrowed.

"I'm going out for a while," he said abruptly, pulling away so quickly she almost lost her balance.

He shoved his feet in his boots and disappeared out into the night without taking his hat or coat.

She managed to keep the kids from eating the candy, promising they could have it in the morning; hopefully it didn't make them hyper for school.

"I need to put these guys to bed," she said to Bob.

"That's fine," he said smoothly, his grin easy. "I can hang out here at the table until you're done."

She nodded, taking the little ones into their bedroom and sending the boys to brush their teeth and shower.

She'd gotten used to Abner helping her. The kids missed him too. Bob was easy to look at, he was a nice guy, and he'd make some lucky girl a great husband, but she really wanted him to leave. She had a man who was better than all the Bobs in the world, and she'd hurt him. Not intentionally but she knew she had nonetheless.

Probably if things were fine between them, Bob being there wouldn't have been that big of a deal. But because of what she'd asked of him and because of how she'd not straightened things up between Abner and her, it had worsened everything.

Finally, she had the children all cleaned up, changed, and tucked in. She closed their door softly and walked into the kitchen where Bob was still sitting at the table and doing something on his phone.

"Can I get you something to drink? Are you hungry?" she asked.

"No, I'm good. I've got a reservation at the next town west of here but figured I'd stop in and say hi."

"I see." She hated to mention the text she'd sent.

He shut his phone off but flipped it over and over in his hand.

"I'm sorry I didn't reply to your emails," he finally said.

She clasped her hands in front of her on the table and looked at them. So, he had gotten them but just ignored her. Figured.

He put one hand over hers, and she froze. It took her three seconds to think to move out from under it, but by then, he had leaned closer.

"I'm sorry. Really, I am. When I offered you a place to stay, you only had three kids." His hand squeezed. "Seriously, Cora, I don't know any man who would be interested in having six kids, even if they were his, living in his house. You do understand this, right?"

His head had lowered, and his eyes were staring into hers.

That's when the door opened and Abner walked in.

Chapter 20

Abner stood in the barn, the familiar smell of musty hay mixing with the tangier scent of old cow manure. He'd decided while Cora was gone that he couldn't make her want to stay with him. Of course he couldn't.

He also realized, quite clearly, at some point he had wanted Cora and her children to be the family he'd always wanted, and maybe he was pushing too hard for what he wanted and not stepping back and allowing her to be what she needed to be. Even if that didn't include him.

Easier said than done, he supposed, since he couldn't stand to see her with Bob.

He might love her, but he also couldn't stand to have her use him again. So when she'd come over and, for the first time, voluntarily put her arm around him, it had taken him a few seconds to realize that it was Stephen all over again, because he wanted it to be real for him.

Yeah, he might love her, but it was easy for that love to feel more like hate when she'd taken everything he'd done and thrown it back in his face.

He hadn't done anything to make her love him, he'd done it because he loved her, but he had to draw the line at her using him.

Except...

Isn't that where he got in trouble before? Thinking that he knew everything and not giving her a chance to explain?

He searched back over his memories, but he just couldn't see any other explanation for this. Everything had to be the way he thought it was.

But that's what he'd thought before. It's what had caused all the years of loneliness and longing for him and pain for Cora.

It took him an hour to come to his senses, but when he did, it wasn't hard to decide what to do.

He opened the door to his home, ready to give his wife whatever support she needed.

But his first look almost made him turn around and walk right back out.

Bob held Cora's hand on the table, and their heads were bent down together like they were sharing secrets.

He closed the door. "Maybe it's time for you to leave." He leveled his gaze at Bob.

Cora stood immediately. "I agree. I wish you the best with everything, and don't worry, I won't ask to stay with you again. I never got to tell you that Abner and I are married."

Bob's head jerked back. His eyes immediately went to Cora's bare left hand.

Abner should have made time to offer her the ring he'd bought. It should have been a priority.

"Hey, well, congratulations." He stood. "Guess some of those kids are his, huh?" He was looking at Cora, but Abner answered.

"All of them are."

He didn't feel like it was a lie. They were going to be as much his as he could make them and Cora would let them be.

"Guess I'll be heading out then," Bob said in the awkward silence that had descended.

Cora didn't say anything when the door closed behind Bob. Eventually, they heard his car start. The lights came on, and he pulled out.

Abner shoved his hands in his pockets, knowing he should apologize but not wanting to at all.

"I'm sorry."

"I'm sorry."

They laughed, a little strained, as their apologies came out together.

He didn't really want to sit at the table where she'd just been with Bob and have a serious discussion with her, but there really wasn't anywhere else.

"Do you have a few minutes?" he asked, feeling more awkward than he wanted to admit to.

"Yes, I really do need to talk to you."

Oh, that's right. She'd said she wanted to talk, and he imagined it wasn't anything good. He could take this. Whatever it was, he could take it.

"Do you want to sit? I can get you a drink."

"How about you sit. And I'll get you something." He went to the sink, trying to keep his hands from shaking, and filled two water glasses.

They clinked as he set them on the table. Even the wind seemed to quit blowing, and silence filled the kitchen.

He pulled a chair out. Not the one that Bob was sitting in. He laid his hand out, palm up, on the table. Asking without words.

She placed hers in it, not hesitating.

Their eyes met. His own uncertainty reflected back to him.

"I did a lot of thinking while I was alone in the hotel room." She breathed deep then lifted her face to meet his eyes.

"I did a lot of thinking while you were gone too." He still didn't know what was going on with Bob and her, but he was encouraged that she didn't fight for Bob to stay or, worse, to go with him. "I can't make you stay."

"You don't have to."

"It's what I want. But I guess I never really told you why."

"You want a family."

"I do. It's one of my dreams. I can't deny it." His thumb stroked over her hand. Her skin soft against the callouses on his thumb. "But that's not the biggest reason."

"Oh?"

"I..." He wanted to rub his hands over his jeans, felt like they were sweating and his pulse was jumping out of his skin. "I fell for you before. All those years ago, that short time we dated, I fell in love with you." Her mouth opened, but he continued before she could say anything. "I was too proud to say so, and you're right, I left, thinking the worst of you, when you didn't deserve it." He swallowed against the tightness in his throat and blew a breath out. "I don't want to make that mistake again. Or any new ones." He smiled a little, but it faded almost immediately. He'd never been more serious. "I love you. It's not contingent on what you decide to do, or where you go, or where you live, or even who you live with. I guess I'm just stubborn and persistent. Because I loved you when you were nineteen and I'll love you when you're ninety and what you do isn't going to change how I feel about you, because it doesn't change who you are."

Her hand came up to cup his cheek. "That was beautiful."

That statement felt like it would have a "but" after it, and he braced himself, even as he pressed his cheek against her warmth.

"I love you, too." She ran her finger over the vein in his hand. "I want to stay. If you'll have me."

"Here?" The word came out, almost a squeak. "Wait. Go back to that last."

"Huh?"

"Where you said you loved me."

"Oh." Her brown eyes sparkled. "I love you."

"Louder?"

She leaned forward. "You want me to wake the kids?"

He had to smile. "I want them to hear it. I want the whole world to hear it."

"I'm sorry, but no one is going to hear it out here where we're at."

He sobered immediately. "Are you going to be able to stay here? You gotta be pretty rugged, and it's isolated, and—"

"Shh." She put a finger on his lips. "I want to be where you are."

Her finger dropped and he missed it immediately.

He tilted his head. "I thought you didn't want to be dependent on a man again?"

"I didn't." She nodded, then sighed. "But when I was at that hotel, alone, I realized that it wasn't just me. That we'd be dependent on each other." She looked at him from under her lashes. "I thought maybe you needed me almost as much as I needed you."

"I'm only half of what I could be without you." It was so true. "I can do it. I can live without you. And if you get that job in Cincinnati, I know I need to let you go. But everything I am is made better when you're with me." He grinned and shrugged. "Plus, life's just more fun when you're around."

"Teasing me does not count."

"It's flirting."

"Really?"

"Yeah. And you give it right back. You know it."

"Well..." She grinned at him, and his heart turned over, like a dog wanting its belly rubbed. "I got the job in Cincinnati."

His insides shriveled, and his smile faded.

Her lips pursed. "They called today. It didn't take me long to tell them I'm not taking it."

It took three seconds for that to sink in. He laughed. "That was not teasing. That was torture."

"No. Torture is you, sitting on your hands and only letting me kiss you once."

"Whoa. I was the one being tortured in that scenario."

She tilted her head. "I guess we could switch places. Then we'd know for sure who was being tortured."

"I'd like to kiss you some, wife." He knew his grin was wolfish. "And I want to touch you while I'm doing it."

"I'm good with that." Her eyes twinkled. "Under one condition."

"I'm not sure I want conditions on this."

"I don't want you sleeping in the barn."

His smile faded. He couldn't stop the jumping of his heart, but what he wanted couldn't supersede what Cora needed.

"I don't want to be like the rest of the men in your life."

Her hand tightened on his. "There's no chance of that. I know I'm dumb and slow at times, but I've known almost from the first that you weren't like the other guys. I'd just made a decision and I was so determined not to screw up again. Plus," her eyes dropped and she studied their joined hands. "I was scared," she whispered.

"No," he hissed, his hand going to her face. He stood, pulling her up. "Don't be scared."

"I'm sorry."

He put his arms around her, wishing he could take her fear.

"I know you're not like them, but I'd made so many bad choices. I didn't trust myself to make another one, and I was so scared that I'd screw up, yet again. Trusting you and being let down would be even worse because of how I feel about you."

His heart pushed against his chest with every strong beat.

"Rationally I knew you would do everything you said you would, but emotionally, my heart was just afraid to trust." Her hands moved over his back and he closed his eyes.

"Was?"

"Yes. I'm not saying I don't have moments of anxiety, but I know we're making the right decision."

"I don't want there to be any anxiety." He took her long ponytail and wrapped his hand around it, tugging gently, pulling her head up to look at him.

"I've done everything so wrong," she whispered.

He shook his head. "We have six beautiful children. They're the silver lining in everything."

She pulled both her lips in and he knew she wasn't completely convinced.

"Let's not look back. We can't fix anything behind us. But we can go forward. Together."

Her lips pursed and her jaw jutted out a little. "Just like that?"

He nodded. "We make the choice. Then we stick to it. Whatever comes, we just stick."

"It sounds easy."

"If we're both holding on, and don't let go, it will be."

She nodded slowly as though thinking about his words. He could almost see the change as she pushed away the last of her fear and decided to trust them. Her body moved. Just a slight shift, but it yanked his heart and sent a shockwave through his veins.

"I think this is where you kiss me," she whispered, looking up.

He swallowed, wanting to, but, "Are you sure? It'll kill me to see regret in your eyes tomorrow morning."

"Then you'd better kiss me, because the only thing I'll regret is you leaving."

His lips curved up as his head lowered. "I guess that means I'm gonna wake up beside you."

Her smile matched his and she tugged his head down. He allowed it, putting his hands around her, feeling her soft curves before his lips touched hers.

It was different than before, more fierce, knowing he didn't have to hold back or pull away because she'd chosen him.

A long time later he lay in the dark in the bedroom that he'd made to be hers, but had become theirs tonight. Her hair lay spread over his chest and he stroked the soft strands, knowing he'd never get tired of feeling it run through his fingers.

Her head lay on his arm and one of her legs was thrown over his, but she wasn't sleeping. Her fingers lightly traced over his ribs and he figured she could do that for about ten years and he wouldn't want her to quit.

He might be sleepy and deliciously tired, but he wouldn't drift off until she stopped. He'd waited years. There was no way he'd miss a second of her touch.

"Abner?"

"Hmm?"

"Thank you."

Well, it didn't sound like regret, anyway, but it confused him a little. "For what?"

"Where most people would look at me and see all my mistakes, you looked at me and saw something worth loving. I'm still not sure I understand it, but thank you."

"We all make mistakes, and we all have reasons for them. You could have hated me forever for walking out on you without giving you a chance to explain." He ran his hand down the soft skin of her arm. "You figured out a way to love me anyway."

She grunted.

A LITTLE BODY LANDED on Cora, startling her from a pretty nice dream. She grunted as a sharp knee pushed into her stomach.

"Why is Mr. Abner in your bed?" Summer asked, standing beside her bed and looking down at her while Luna crawled across her to Abner.

Cora blinked once, before sitting straight up, clutching the blanket to her chest. "I never set the alarm. Oh, rats. You guys are going to be late for school."

Abner's big, rough hand landed on the small of her back. "Relax. I'll drive them in. It'll be fine."

"I can't believe I forgot."

"I can." She could hear the smile in his voice and she turned, looking over her shoulder at her husband. The covers were pulled up to his waist, thankfully, and Luna bounced on his chest, her dark curls bouncing.

"You are not allowed to flirt with me when I've forgotten to set the alarm and my kids are going to be late for school."

"I think that's the perfect time to flirt."

"Mom?"

Her head swiveled, and she clutched the covers tighter. Andrew, holding Claire, and Derrick stood in the doorway.

Cora hadn't even heard that Claire was up. Usually she babbled to herself in her crib, and Cora must have slept right through it.

It'd been pretty late until she'd fallen asleep.

"Yes, dear?" she said to Andrew who had his brows drawn together, like he was puzzled.

"Does this mean Mr. Abner is our new dad?"

"Are we staying here?" Kohlton asked before she could answer Andrew, pushing between his two older brothers and coming to stand beside Summer.

Abner shifted beside her, then his chest pressed, warm and hard, against her back as he leaned on his hand behind her.

"Your mom said you were staying." Abner spoke for her. It hurt that she'd been so messed up that her kids knew what a new man could mean. "And yes, I'm taking responsibility for all of you, so I guess that makes me the dad around here."

His head dropped, and his words were soft in her ear. "You told me you weren't going to regret this."

She shook herself. "No. I don't. It just makes me sad that I've messed my kids up," she whispered back.

"That's the last time."

Andrew came over. Claire held out her hands and Cora took her with one arm, the other still clutching the blanket.

"So, we can call you dad?" Andrew asked, still looking unsure.

"Can if you want," Abner said easily as Claire wiggled her chubby little body over to him, and Luna clung tight with her arms around his neck.

Andrew's face cleared, but Derrick crossed his arms. "How long are you staying?"

"'Til I die. That's what I promised, and that's what I meant."

He didn't look convinced.

Kohlton had worked his way onto the bed and Summer climbed on, too. Cora lay back, tired of fighting to keep the covers up, and snuggled Summer along one side of her with Kohlton squeezing down between Abner and her.

"You two might as well pile on too," Abner said to Derrick and Andrew. "Looks like breakfast is going to have to wait."

"But school can't."

Abner stretched over Kohlton and kissed her forehead. "We'll get them to school." He grinned. "In a bit."

Epilogue

Angela looked up from her Sunday School classroom. The hall just got a lot noisier and, sure enough, Abner Coblantz stood holding Luna with little Kohlton gripping his hand tight. His wife, Cora, bounced a baby on her hip while she said something to her older boys. Probably telling them to be good or else.

Angela smiled. Since they'd moved here from Ohio, her Sunday School class size had doubled. She had the dubious privilege of teaching the preschoolers. Really, most of the time she loved it, but it definitely wasn't a job for the faint of heart.

But she'd grown up in church and she could handle anything a three or four year old could throw at her.

She hoped.

Abner waved at her from her classroom doorway as he dropped his children off. She lifted a hand in acknowledgement, her focus on making Kohlton feel welcome.

Except her eye caught on the figure that stood behind Abner.

Mack, from the harvest crew.

It wasn't that she particularly liked him. He was just one of Clay's crew. But it was odd to see him carrying children. A boy and a girl.

Strange, since she hadn't realized he was married. She'd only ever seen him at "work" so she didn't know what his life was like where he lived the rest of the year. One of the flat states. Kansas or Oklahoma or something.

She'd always loved seeing a man who was good with children, and Mack held them like he was used to it, while both kids clung to his neck like they were comfortable with him.

Was he their dad?

She walked back to her doorway on the pretense of getting Kohlton settled and glanced around quickly as Abner greeted him. He didn't seem to be with a woman, although his wife could be anywhere.

Just because she didn't see her didn't mean he didn't have one. Although, she took one more quick glance. No. She didn't see a ring.

It wasn't like she could care.

She'd always been focused on Clay and didn't really know Mack well enough to know much of anything about him. But he'd been there when things had gone down with Clay and Boone, and wouldn't be interested in her anyway. So she turned her back and bent over the table, helping Kohlton and the other little boy to get crayons out and start to color.

Her ear was tuned to the door, though, because both of the children in Mack's arms looked like they'd be in her class if he was going to drop them off.

She wanted to think she'd learned a lot about herself and had grown through the mistakes she'd made this past summer, but she couldn't expect the people who'd witnessed her nasty actions to think anything but poorly of her. That included Mack. This was as good of a time as any to start trying to sway his opinion.

She took a deep breath and straightened, hoping with all her heart that she could begin today changing the trajectory of the rest of her life.

THANK YOU SO MUCH FOR reading! If you enjoyed it, I'd love for you to leave a review.

The next book in the series, *The Cowboy's Mistletoe Christmas* is available HERE[1].